'THE CHESS GAME'

Sometimes winning isn't everything.

By
Donald L. Boone

IFPublications
mgn.editor@gmail.com

Other books written by Donald Boone

Chess Records

Chess Histories And Mysteries

Chess Stories Through The Ages

Chess Tales Of Kings And Queens

Mastering Basic Chess

The Chess Set

The Chess Game

The Scholastic Chess Coach

Those Who Play Chess

THE CHESS GAME

Frank Chambers, had acquired the habit of reading the newspaper each morning before he went to work. He especially enjoyed the personals column, and it had become his favorite. On a recent morning he happened to read about a chess move in the personals column. He'd been surprised to find it listed there. Then he began finding a chess move listed in this part of the paper every other week.

His curiosity rose each time because these were chess moves apparently being made by only one player, and he knew this was only one side of the game. He began to look for them each morning thereafter. An answering chess move never seemed to appear. As a police detective he also noticed that coincidentally someone died in what was believed to be an accidental death each time one of these chess moves appeared in the newspaper.

As his suspicions begin to mount concerning the accidental deaths, he took a chance and started to play opposing chess moves against the advertised moves in the newspaper. He did this by placing a corresponding ad in the paper himself. Each time he did this, what he began to suspect may be murders, stopped. The occurrence, which had been taking place every two weeks, and the regularity of the deaths, had changed. Frank found that when he thwarted a move in the newspaper's chess game, no one died that week, giving the community two more weeks of safety against the deadly chess player.

As Frank Chambers narrows his leads to what he thinks is the killer's identity, it appears his primary suspect has already died. Frank finally issued a chess game challenge to the player in the newspaper.

Having arranged with the newspaper to keep his real identity secret, he receives a telephone call. An arrangement is made to meet and to play a game of chess across the board.

As the killer nears the end of his list of victims, his anger, and curiosity leads him to succumb to the temptation of playing a game against his latest tormentor. After all, no one can possibly know what he's been doing.

R	N	B	Q	K	B	N	R
P	P	P	P	P	P	P	P
P	*P*	*P*	*P*	*P*	*P*	*P*	*P*
R	*N*	*B*	*Q*	*K*	*B*	*N*	*R*

THE CHESS GAME

Harvey Eldridge sat quietly, though he was tense. The chess competition elimination games had dragged on for days. The games themselves didn't take that long, but with the social parties going on, they only played chess during the mornings and early afternoons.

The competition had been stiff, and nerves were frayed with most of the players who had completed their games, but now, today, he was sitting across the board from Richard Evans. The final game was in play, and the boat's main deck salon was heavy with the smell of cigarette and cigar smoke. Even with the air conditioning going, and the glass sliding door open, the room was hot and humid.

Harvey had waited seven years to play this opening against an opponent who seemed unaware of the trap being set on the chessboard. He had opened with the standard Sicilian opening, then carefully turned it to the Blackburn trap. Originally was known as the "Legal Opening" His opponent, Richard Evans, continued to move his own pieces in such a manner that would bring Harvey's swindle to fruition and pull Evans into making the critical losing move and the match. He almost felt guilty, because if Evans fell for the trap, it would be a short game.

As Evans watched Eldridge's hands faltering, as if trying to decide which move to make, he was remembering each of the games that had led him to this very chair. Each game he'd played in the eliminations had been tough, each one more competitive than the one before.

But the results were such that the elimination match games had led him to this point in his life. This game, of all the games, was the one that each player had played for. The pressure on him was grueling, and it had been a long and drawn out day.

Harvey had, had very little to drink today, other than lemonade, and he knew his opponent was only drinking iced tea. Both players wanted to keep their wits about them and were avoiding alcohol. The remaining players were watching the game in play. They reminded Harvey of vultures waiting for the scraps after the kill, and they were also consuming liquor as if there was no tomorrow. A few were really using it to release all of the tension that had built in them during the elimination series. In a sense there would be no tomorrow, because tonight, with the tournament over, the 'Largo' would slip her mooring lines and start the return trip to Seattle Washington.

As Harvey reached for one of his chess pieces, someone nearby dropped a glass and it had shattered on the floor. To make such a disturbing noise in the room at this time, was nearly unforgivable as it could easily distract the two players left who were in the depths of serious thought. Everyone had looked at the person responsible, including himself and Richard Evans, his opponent. When they looked back at the chessboard, one of Harvey's fingers was seen resting on his King's Knight which was on the King's Bishop three square. Immediately he looked at the game referee, and he too had seen Harvey's fingers touch his King's Knight.

Everyone knew that tournament rules are such, that a piece having been touched had to be moved, regardless the cost to the offending player in the game. Now, Harvey had to move the Knight. He had intended to move this piece anyway, but now he could make it look as if he had made a mistake. An error on his part, and everyone knew that an error in a championship game could bring the end soon after. He moved the Knight.

Now it was Richard's turn again. He had been trying to decide which chess piece to use next, and he had to make his move before the chess clock's time ran out. Richard had considering one of three different moves. Now, however, he couldn't understand why his opponent had made such a blundering move with his white Knight. He thought it could have been moved to a better position, but perhaps Harvey had decided that to capture a black Pawn was better than nothing.

Richard's eyes were now glued to his Queen's Bishop. The apparent blunder Harvey had made with his move would allow him to capture Harvey's Queen, a major piece of power in the game. He knew that to capture the opposing Queen would cost him a Bishop, a small price to pay, but if the clock ran out before he made his next move, it wouldn't make any difference as the game would be over by default.

Every player's eyes were watching him, waiting for his next move. He sipped his iced drink slowly trying to act nonchalant. Then he returned the glass to the table slowly, so as to control his hand. Surely it would betray his nervousness.

He was keenly aware game time was slipping by quickly. Tension in the room was thick, as if each movement of the second hand on the chess clock on the table between the two men could be felt.

Richard had won the first match game, then his opponent, Harvey, had won the next one. This game was the last one to be played. The final game in the two out of three, was a chess death match. The winner would take all, the prize was high, and to him it meant a great deal more. To him the prize money meant survival.

Harvey was squirming in his chair. It seemed as if he was trying hard not to make any noise, but his intention was indeed a false ploy to distract his opponent. Then he saw what he had been waiting for, the very move he had been anticipating. The move of greed. The seeming blundering move with his Knight was about to pay off.

Richard's watery eyes were bothering him, they were irritated with the smoke and fatigue of the long day, he had a pounding headache and the game was intense. He glanced at the clock that was quickly ticking away his needed game time. Reaching up he slid the palm of his hand across his forehead to remove the sweat. His other hand instinctively reached out and picked up the opposing white Queen, intending to replace it with his black Bishop.

The Queen had just barely cleared the surface of the chessboard, you probably couldn't have seen the space under it, but to even touch it, was the same effect. He quickly set the chess piece back down in the same spot from where he had picked it up, hoping no

4

one would notice what he had done. Now, he was very upset with himself, and it was because of the damn 'Touch move rule,' he and the rest of the group of players had agreed to play by.

He had seen the error of his move but not until after he had picked up the opposing Queen. The greed to take the white Queen had been a very heavy temptation. At first it appeared as if the Queen was almost free for the taking. It appeared as though he could capture the opposing Queen and only lose a Bishop in the exchange. Then the horror of the error had come to him, and it came too late. He knew the cost of capturing the Queen was much higher than that of a mere Bishop.

It grew deathly quiet in the room now as everyone waited in anticipation. No one moved, or made a noise. All of them who saw him put the Queen back down, were now watching the referee. Most of them knew what had happened, because everyone had been watching the game intently. If not from the bar, they would be watching a closed circuit television somewhere on the boat, and nearly every chess player knew what the results of the error he'd made had to be, the trap he had fallen into.

The referee had seen Richard Evans touch Harvey Eldridge's Queen, then replace it on the Queen's square. He had paused a few seconds to see if Evans would voluntarily finish the move. When he did not, the referee stood slowly, put the remains of his ice cold beer down, and quietly moved away from his observation chair. When he reached the game table, he spoke to Richard directly, quietly, but in a firm and gentle voice.

"I'm sorry Mr. Evans, but having touched the Queen, if at all possible you must capture her according to the rules of the game, sir."

"Yes. Yes, of course," Richard answered. It seemed an eternity before he finished making the move he had started to make previously. His left hand seemed to weigh a thousand pounds as he moved it to pluck the white Queen from the original white Queen one square. His own black Bishop was now residing on that space next to the white King. He knew his offending Bishop would not be taken, and it would sit on that square in shame.

There was no question, nearly everyone knew he had lost the game when he captured the Queen. A few of the players remaining at the long mahogany bar did not realize what the outcome would be from this point in the game's standing. They, too, were unfamiliar with the Lega'l opening. Those that were aware of this trap, were also aware of the impending doom that lay ahead, a few starting to whisper the answer to the others, "It's mate in two."

Richard's legs felt weak, but he summoned some inner strength, and with an air of elegance he stood slowly, reached down and tipped his King on its side. A sign that he was resigning the game to his opponent. Harvey stood, and reached his hand out in gratitude. "Thank you, Mr. Evans."

Richard took his hand. "Of course." He continued with a short congratulation to his opponent on the good game, as if it was an everyday event. Then he walked quietly to the bar and asked for a bourbon and water with two aspirins.

Of the group of men standing around who had been watching the game closely, those who were familiar with this particular chess game opening continued explaining to the others how the white pieces would checkmate the black King in two moves. A few had drawn chess boards on bar napkins to emphasize the end result. Harvey had won the grand prize of one million dollars, his opponent Richard, would win nothing.

Richard had been in serious financial trouble before and this was to be his way out. His anger, just barely under control, was hard to hide. He left the group quickly, and went to his cabin. Inside the privacy of his own stateroom, he sat on the edge of the bed. His head lowered down into his hands and tears began to well up as he thought of how much ruin his life was now facing.

That evening, as Harvey lay on the stateroom's bed, the minuscule vibrations of large diesel engines could be felt as the large yacht moved through the dark waters. He was playing the tape of the recorded championship game on the VCR on the guest's television set in his stateroom. He was ecstatic about having won the game, and he was mildly surprised that the opening he played had not been recognized by his opponent.

He also knew that most serious players would have related it to the 1922 World Championship game in Budapest, or the history of Henry Blackburn. When he dropped off to sleep, the check for one million dollars remained clutched between his finger tips.

HAROLD CHILDES

Harold was enjoying the last of the daylight's warmth. The sun's rays shining on the surface of the water looked like a bouquet of various colored roses. The reflections dancing off the water's surface seemed like sparkling diamonds of rose quartz. Slowly he meandered through his flower garden savoring the last of the nearly perfect day. He stopped to finger the Fire Cracker Fuchsia growing under the protection of one large Madrona tree close to the edge of his unfenced property on the bluff.

Tilting his head, he marveled at the Fuchsia's red and pink colors. *'Not many of this kind around.'* Then he walked to the edge of his property where he stood looking down at the rocky beach far below him. It was a view that evoked a feeling of fear in him, but occasionally drew him to this spot. Suddenly, he became aware of someone standing behind him. Startled, he turned to look, and upon seeing whom it was, said. "Oh. Hello. My gosh, I haven't seen you in some time."

His visitor said, "No, you haven't." Then after some hesitation he continued. "I was driving in the area and just thought I'd stop by for a quick visit."

Though he had no intention of leaving until he finished what he had come for, he added apologetically, "I'm sorry if I'm interrupting, I can. . ."

Relaxing from the startling interruption, Harold said "No. No, you're not interrupting anything." Although Harold couldn't figure out why this man would be coming to see him, he said, "Your welcome."

Turning away at a slight angle Harold pointed out toward the view. "Wonderful, isn't it?"

His surprise guest stepped closer saying, "It sure is." Then after a few brief seconds of looking at the view with Harold, and after he had glanced quickly around the area surrounding the back yard he added, "How far is it down to the beach from up here?"

"I'm not really sure." Harold said. Then he stepped through some small shrubbery, inching closer to the edge as if to measure the distance by eye.

The feeling of his landing at the bottom of the bluff only lasted momentarily.

The Pawn took two steps forward

R	N	B	Q	K	B	N	R
P	P	P	P	P	P	P	P
			$\mathcal{P}$				
$\mathcal{P}$	$\mathcal{P}$	$\mathcal{B}$	$\mathcal{P}$		$\mathcal{P}$	$\mathcal{P}$	$\mathcal{P}$
$\mathcal{R}$	$\mathcal{N}$	$\mathcal{B}$	$\mathcal{Q}$	$\mathcal{K}$	$\mathcal{B}$	$\mathcal{N}$	$\mathcal{R}$

P-K4

FIRST MONDAY IN SEPTEMBER

Frank Chambers, following his usual morning routine, had already showered and shaved and was sitting at his kitchen table reading the morning paper before he left the apartment. Much of this habit he'd acquired when he made detective six years earlier.

Finished with reading what he referred to as the educational pages, which were the comics, and as he was about to put the paper down, he remembered he hadn't read one of his favorite sections of the paper, the personal ads. He read this section of the paper because of the unusual things people would say about themselves, or comments they would make in an attempt to attract someone else into their lives.

The pages rustled as he turned them one at a time. When he came to the page he wanted, he started reading down the column. He stopped at one ad that said "Married woman looking for a friend to talk with." It went on to give somewhat of a description of her and a P.O.Box number. *'Oh sure,'* he thought. *'Just someone to talk with. Well. . .it could happen.'*

Getting up from his small kitchen table, Frank went to the stove and poured himself another cup of hot coffee. The steam rose from the cup and into the still air of the kitchen. Then he again settled in his favored spot at the table. Though his chairs were hardback chairs, they were comfortable. Frank had placed cushions on each one just for added comfort. He picked up his coffee cup, and was just about to take a sip, when his eyes caught sight of the next ad in the paper.

He stopped, his cup still on its way to his lips as he read the ad, and then he read it again. His coffee remained in the cup, but lapped at the edge, begging to spill the hot liquid onto his lap.

The ad simply read, "P-K4."

Deeper in thought now, Frank murmured, "Hummm, Pawn to King's four." Frank was having a problem understanding why an opening chess move would be in this section of the paper. He was trying to think back, and he couldn't recall a chess section in this paper anywhere, ever.

The only time this paper carried anything about chess, was when a notable chess match was going on somewhere in the world, and was pitting two of the world's Grand Masters against one another. Sometimes even then it wouldn't have anything about the championship chess game in the paper. Yet there it was, an opening chess move.

He also knew it was from a chess player who had been playing for some time. He knew this because it was written in the old version of writing chess moves, rather than the newer algebraic method. He too, was of the older school.

THE FERRY

Marty reached out in the darkness, his hand searching through the air for the source of the aggravating noise. Finding the alarm button, he pushed it to stop the irritation. He lay quietly for a few minutes with his eyes still closed. The thick quilt was pulled over his ear to keep it warm while he lay on his side. Sadly, though he was enjoying the comfort and warmth of the seemingly large and empty bed, it didn't contain his life's mate.

Today, he planned on going out to the island to check on the old house where he and Gladys had spent so many happy years together. He still missed her very much. Even yet, when he was working on some project, or on any little thing, he still automatically asked her to hand him some tool he needed. She had always been by his side and helped him this way when she could. His mind again wandered to the thought, *'Maybe I should just sell the damn place. Don't use it anymore, unless one of the children comes home during their vacations.'*

He finally forced himself to get up, and ambled into the cold bathroom to shave and shower. He hadn't completely closed the bedroom window the night before because she liked fresh air at night, and because of Gladys he'd gotten into the same sleeping habit. At the last minute he decided to skip his morning shower, he just didn't feel up to taking the time. After he finished his morning coffee and toast, Marty put the dishes in the kitchen sink. Leaving them to be dealt with later he went out to the garage, closing and locking the duplex door behind him.

As he climbed into the old car, he pushed his attaché case over onto the passenger seat. He only carried the case around with him out of habit these days, he kept whatever book he was reading at the time in it as well. He pushed the key into the ignition switch and started the car. Opening the automatic garage door, he backed out, closing the garage door after him.

After leaving the duplex, Marty drove down the old road coming from the northeast and passed the log holding area in the shallow bay. Its logs were nearly depleted from the heavy usage during the past few months by the local pulp mill, and the stench of the mud flats irritated his nose. Just as he approached the marina, he turned right heading toward the parking area near the yacht club and the ferry dock.

As soon as he got out of the car Marty knew he hadn't dressed warmly enough. This had been the first really cold morning in some time. The weather had been very nice lately, but now the season was beginning to show a coming change. Then to top it off he had arrived earlier than he would have normally.

When he walked down the dock ramp, and arrived at the small ferry, the steps that should be in place for boarding the ferry, were missing. He'd been able to get aboard the ferry without the steps, but he had to struggle to do it. He labored to get one knee up on the steel deck then pulled himself aboard by holding onto the railing. As he panted from the effort, he reached for the sliding door,

'Thank God the door to the main cabin is unlocked,' though he had expected it to be, and the electrical shore power was turned on as well.

14

Once he was inside the main cabin, with the sliding door closed behind him, he put his attaché case down on one of the benches. Still chilled and shivering, he turned on the electric bulkhead heater. Moving slowly around inside the cold steel cabin, he moved to the metal cabinet where the electric coffeepot was kept on top behind a fiddle rail. He plugged in the large coffeepot, and set the switch to the highest heat level. The pot had been ready to start, as the coffee grounds had been previously measured and dumped into the perforated metal basket. The water was up to the thirty cup mark and only required the electrical cord to be plugged in and the switch to be turned on.

It seemed to take forever, but Marty had finally gotten warm. He had a longer wait than usual this morning because he had gotten here so early. Leaning over he lifted the top of a passenger seat up, its hinges squeaking as the top rotated up and away from him. In the storage area under the lid he rummaged through the various cushions until he found five of them that suited his needs.

He let them drop to the steel floor at his feet. He put the lid back down, and placed the cushions next to each other all in a row on top of the hard seat. Moving his attaché against the cabin's outer bulkhead, Marty lay down, stretching out on the cushions.

The coffee began to percolate quietly, its rich aroma filling the cabin around him. He knew it would turn off automatically when the coffee was done. The cabin lights were too bright and bothered his eyes, yet he didn't want to turn them off, and there wasn't any way to turn them down.

He raised up, reached down to the other end of the bench he was on, and picked up a section of yesterday's newspaper that had been left by a previous passenger.

After lying back down on the cushions, he put the folded sheet of newspaper over his eyes affording him some darkness. The smell of dampness wafted gently from the piece of paper now covering his face. He made some allowance for the smell as the price for the darkness it afforded his eyes.

It seemed as if he'd barely drifted off to sleep, though he knew some kind of time had passed. Suddenly he heard, or at least became aware of something or someone outside the ferry's cabin. He sat up as he'd been expecting the ferry's skipper to arrive any time.

He listened intently, then heard someone call from outside the cabin where he waited. "What the . . . " Thinking someone needed a hand getting aboard, he got up stiffly, and slid the cold steel door open. Looking down he was surprised to see who was standing on the dock.

"Give me a hand up will ya?"

Marty offered his hand as the newcomer had asked. And as Marty tried to help the man get onboard, he knew his own footing was precarious on the damp deck as he reached down.

Suddenly, he slipped and fell. He had been pulled sideways by the weight of the other man's body, and then Marty's head hit the side of the dock. The large cast iron mooring cleat on the dock only knocked him unconscious at first, but Marty never recovered from the blow. His bulky body was shoved over the edge of the dock by the very person he'd attempted to help. Marty never felt the cold as it enveloped him.

Finished with his intended task, the other man now replaced the loosened aft mooring line back onto the dock cleat. He looked around quickly. With his arm extended as far as he was able to reach, he got a hold on the bottom of the steel sliding door above him. He quickly shoved the door closed. Satisfied no one had seen him. He walked away toward the nearby parking area. 'That went well.'

MARTY HANSON

Frank arrived at the county office building just after seven thirty. The morning seemed fairly warm, yet the weather forecast was for a light rain later in the day. As usual, he parked his car in the under ground parking lot reserved for the sheriff's office personnel. Frank's space was vacant, which it was supposed to be, but often wasn't. Sometimes, someone from his office would be in such a hurry that they parked in each other's spots. It was a friendly, but ongoing war over their personal parking places.

He had once parked in Jim Parson's spot in a rush to get to his office for some information. It was information that was supposed to be a good lead regarding a case he had been working on. When he had come back for his car less than twenty minutes later, he found his car chained and padlocked to a nearby cement pillar. He'd had to get the building maintenance man to bring some bolt cutters to get his car free of the pillar. Jim had sworn he wasn't the one to do it, but Frank wasn't sure he believed him. Since then he and Jim had become good friends, often working as a team on cases.

Frank crossed the open parking area feeling the chilly breeze blowing through the underground area. Its construction design allowed air to funnel through like a small wind tunnel. He approached the elevator, pushed the up button, and waited patiently.

When the doors opened, two uniformed police officers got off and headed toward their patrol car, which would be parked in the outer lot. As they passed each other, Frank said, "Morning fella's."

Both nodded, and answered, "Morning Frank."

Frank got on the elevator, and pushed the button for the third floor. Out of habit he leaned against the back of the elevator,s padded walls. The doors opened at the first floor, and Cary Ann, the computer department supervisor, got on the elevator with him.

He smiled as he heard her say, "Morning Frank." It seemed a warm greeting, and he enjoyed the sound of her voice. He also enjoyed her being near him.

He thought her voice sounded almost musical. "Morning, Cary Ann. How's it goin?" He tried to get closer when he smelled the flowery scent of her morning shower.

"Oh fine." She started to move away out of habit, but stopped, and let him move closer. She wanted the conversation to continue. "They hired two new secretaries, and they seem to think that I work for them. I'm sure you know how that is."

"Yes, I do, but without you running the show in the computer department, not much would get done on time around here, and I'd never get my daily reports." He didn't mean to come across so business like, it just came out that way. He was aware that Cary Ann had been a parole officer for seven years, before she applied for, and was promoted to head the computer section for the police department. Her professional abilities and her personal drive helped her attain this position.

Arriving at the third floor Cary Ann got off first, smiled at him, then turned to the left and headed for her office. Frank watched her walk away from him, marveling at how nice it was to watch her, knowing only a woman could walk that way.

Frank then turned right, and in so doing, he could see through the open doorway at the end of the hall. His partner, Jim Parson, was already at work.

Their desks were pushed up against one another in the small but cramped office the two of them shared with two other detectives. The walls were in bad need of paint, and Frank had put in several requests to have them painted, yet they remained this way.

He and Jim had the office to themselves most of the time. The other two detectives were generally working undercover during the night shift and were rarely at their desks during the day. On occasion, Frank or Jim, would find a note asking one, or both of them, to do something that the other two detectives could not do at night.

Frank pulled his jacket off inside the office, and for once he hung it up on a nearby coat rack with Jim's overcoat. Walking around the side of Jim's desk he pulled the old oak rolling chair out from his desk and sat down. He thought he had the only chair like it in the building, its high armrests affording him comfort at any angle he might be sitting. Frank tried to keep his desk in some kind of order, whereas Jim's was always neat, as was Jim. Frank found a file folder on the top of his desk, a file folder he knew had not been there on Friday.

"This yours, Jim?"

"Humm?.... Oh, no it's about something that happened Saturday morning. The captain of a small ferry between Everett and Gedney Island, found a body in the water between the ferry and the dock. One of his regular customers, I think. Anyway, the harbor master called the cops. There weren't any detectives around at the time, so the uniforms handled it."

"And the body is?"

"They took it to the Everett morgue."

"Anyone check on it yet."

"Nope, they weren't sure who would handle it so they left it for us, and my calendar is flooded today and tomorrow."

"Okay, I'll check it out."

Frank finished some paper work that needed his attention, work that he had left undone from the Friday before. The main item that needed to be done was his monthly report. When he finished writing the report, he locked his shoulder holster with its nine-millimeter automatic pistol in the bottom drawer of his metal desk. He hated to carry a gun, but there were many occasions when he had to. Sometimes departmental policy dictated his being armed. He pulled his jacket on, and turned toward Jim saying,

"Jim, I'm heading for the morgue, if anyone comes looking for me."

"Okay, pardner." Jim never even looked up. His pen was still writing a report.

The county morgue was only a short distance away, the weather still held promise, and Frank decided to walk the short distance even though the morning air smelled like rain. Frank, being from the country, was aware of this smell, although it was a little different being in the city. The city itself wasn't really a large city as far as cities go, it was actually small. Boeing Aircraft was responsible for a large portion of the city's income, and the Navy was in the process of developing property in the area as well.

Frank pushed open the heavy glass double doors of the city office building, which housed the morgue in the basement. When he passed the bulletin board which had civil service jobs listed, he stopped to look them over. Scanning it quickly, he decided there wasn't any other job that seemed inviting to him, though he would take a transfer to a smaller town.

He'd often considered getting into another line of work but also knew he would have a hard time ever finding anything that could replace the enjoyment he often experienced from what he was doing now, nor one that offered the personal freedom it allowed. Frank turned, then walked over to the stairwell. He walked down the gleaming marble stairway to the lower floor.

At the bottom of the stairs he came across Joe Knolles who had been working here for thirty-eight years as the custodian. Joe was humming some song from the blues and was busily running a floor polishing machine over the last of the long corridor. The machine's long orange electrical cord was snaking across the floor.

"What'cha step, Mista Chambas, Suh," Joe said politely as he continued working on the floor.

"Will do. How's the wife doing these days, Joe?" He liked Joseph.

"Well, she's kin'a slow these days. Yuh know, what with her stove up joints an' all."
"Tell her I wish her well, okay?"

"Yessuh." Joe knew every detective in the department and most of the uniformed police officers as well. They all liked him, and his casual southern manner. At Christmas most of them would give him a small gift of some kind.

Frank walked through the door marked County Coroner's Office. Inside the office, a young woman with dark brown hair sat behind her desk working at a computer console. She looked up very briefly when Frank first entered the door, then her head bent back down to the task at hand. He had barely registered in her mind.

"Can I help you?" She asked without looking up again.

"Yes. I'm Frank Chambers from the detective's division of the Sheriff's Office."

"Oh, I'm sorry, Mr. Chambers, I didn't recognize you right away." Her face again turned to see him.

"No problem. I'd like to see the coroner about the body found at the Everett Marina on Saturday."

"Sure. Just a moment please."

She got up from her desk, then disappeared through another door behind her. A few minutes later she reappeared with Victor Hastings, the county-elected coroner. Victor was a small wiry man, short, with black receding hair and wire rim glasses.

"Morning, Frank, come on in." Frank and all the detectives were in this man's realm often, so they all knew one another on a professional basis. Some were personal friends with Victor, often having dinner or playing golf with him. Frank wasn't one of that group.

Frank followed Victor back through the door. They passed by a couple of smaller rooms off the hallway and through two more swinging doors into the main large open room of the coroner's lab. The cold storage lockers that housed the bodies awaiting disposal, whatever their destiny might be, were on the left side of the room. Sometimes they would be here a few days, sometimes longer.

"You're here about the body found at the marina Saturday, are you not?"

"Yessir."

Victor Hastings walked over to the bank of cold storage drawers, read a paper nameplate, then pulled the drawer open. As he slid it open, Frank moved closer so he could see the body better. Victor pulled the sheet back exposing the head and upper torso of an older man who appeared to be about sixty to sixty-five. The body seemed a little bloated, which wasn't unusual. Speaking softly Victor indicated with his finger, an area on the left side of the skull above the left eye that showed some depression as if the head had been struck, or had struck some object. "That led to his death, but you'll find it in my report,"

Frank carefully looked the body over a few minutes, then looked at Victor who said, "I've got a full report on my desk, Frank. Let's go have a look."

They entered Victor's office and he motioned for Frank to sit in the chair placed along side his desk.

"Here's the report. It's pretty standard. He lived in Mukilteo. The family would like to take charge of his body as soon as it's been released. The sooner the better, if you've no objection."

"How'd he die?"

"The first suspicion was drowning. But he didn't drown."

"The blow to the head did him under I'd guess." Frank added.

"Yes, that's how it appears to me. There was very little water in his lungs. He could have hit his head on some protrusion on the steel hull of the ferry, or on the metal cleat on the dock. The cleat was mentioned in the police report. Odds are he fell into the water between the ferry and the dock, his body would then be trapped there until it was found."

"What's your opinion then, Doc?"

"Well, he didn't actually drown. I suspect hypothermia played a large part in his death. From what I understand about the situation, it's probably an accidental death."

Frank read the report, then pulled his notebook out of his jacket pocket to make his own notes. His notebook, a leather bound four by six-inch book, was one he could add pages to if need be. He'd kept his own mini-case files in this book for years. Now he added a new case to it pages.

Frank knew only too well that he might never have need for this information, but on more than one occasion the files he kept in this book had served him well.

Harold Childes, Caucasian / Male. Discovered in the water of the marina by the Captain of the Gedney Island ferry. The body was wedged between the dock and the Ferry's steel hull. It appears he fell overboard, and was an accidental death, cause of death attributed to hypothermia.

FERRY SKIPPER

After leaving the coroner's office, Frank checked an
unmarked car out of the motor pool and drove to the
Everett Marina. He passed the commercial fishing
docks, the small shops for electronics and custom
wood products, then turned down the street where he
would pass between the boat yards and the marina
basin.

He was always amazed at how many boats were in the
yard and being worked on by owners or yard
personnel. Some seemed as though they had been
here in the boatyard forever. Gaping holes where
planks were in the process of being replaced, the
wood often weathered to silver gray as if forgotten.
Paint buckets were found on the ground under a few
hulls. Tarpaulins were covering open areas on many
boat hulls.

Frank didn't get down here to the marina often, but he
was sure he'd seen some of these boats here the last
time he had been here. He parked his car in the
northwest parking lot near the yacht club building.
Locking the car, more out of habit than anything, he
walked down the slanting ramp to 'A' dock. When he
reached the bottom of the ramp, he turned right toward
the fuel dock. He was heading toward the Gedney
Island ferry, which was side tied to the end of the
dock. He was aware it was kept here between runs out
to the island. He found Tom Schaefer, the skipper, on
board.

"Hello, aboard." He said as he climbed up the steps to get aboard. Ducking his head down to clear the metal doorway entrance as he entered the small and sparsely furnished cabin area. Its unadorned walls glared with fresh white paint.

The captain, Tom Schaefer turned toward him, his graying blond hair falling across his forehead. A large hand came up to push the hair away from his ruddy face, then, "The ferry isn't due to go out to the island for another couple of hours yet."

"No problem, I'm not going out to the island. I'm Frank Chambers. I'm with the sheriff's department," he offered his hand, and his identification. The identification went unseen.

"How can I help you Mr. Chambers?"

"Just a couple of questions if you have the time?"

"Sure."

"Were you the skipper on duty, Saturday, when the body was found in the water along side the ferry?"

"Yessir. That's me. I'm the only skipper on this run."

Frank made a mental note of that fact, then asked. "Any thing unusual about the situation that you may have noticed, other than the body that is."

"No, not really. . . Well, yes. The steps to get aboard the ferry were missing. I'm guessing he could'a fallen in the water while he was trying to get back down on the dock from up here." He indicated the outer deck that Frank had just crossed over.

"Get back down on the dock?" Frank asked curiously.

"Yessir. Mr. Childes had already been on board for a while, and maybe had to go to the bathroom at one of the public bathrooms up there," he said, pointing up to the parking area.

"Or he could'a been heading up to his car for somethin."

"How do you know he'd been on board?"

"Oh, he was aboard, all right. He had some cushions laid out on one of the benches as if he was going to take a quick nap. And I found his attaché case against the wall over there. Also, he'd made the coffee."

"Do you still have the attaché case?"

"No sir. The police officer that came by to investigate in the beginning took the attaché case with him. I have a receipt here for it some place if you need it."

Frank made a mental note of it. "No, I don't need it, thanks." Then thinking a moment, he added, "I had steps to climb aboard with when I got here."

"Yeah, you did. The fuel dock people found them floating on the other side of the dock. They were down near the end of the fuel dock when they came to work later that morning. They helped me get'em back."

"How'd the steps end up in the drink?"

"Kids probably."

Frank pulled his small notebook from his right-hand jacket pocket and a pen from his shirt pocket. He started some brief notes for later reference including one about looking for the attaché case, and the officers involved.

"You don't keep the ferry locked then?"

"Normally, yes."

"How was it he was able to get inside when he got aboard?"

"Mr. Childes had a habit of being here the first Saturday morning of every month. He'n his wife had a home out on Gedney Island. I mean, he still has it. Although his wife passed away a few years ago."

"I want to be sure I understand. You're saying that he doesn't live on the Island full time now?"

"That's right. He's got a place up on the hill to the north a bit, but I figure he was only going out to spend the day at the house. He did this about once a month on average. He just goes out to be sure every thing is okay, then he would come back in with me on the last run at the end of the day."

"Know anything about his personal life?"

"Not much more than what I've told you. Some a his neighbors out on the island might know more."

Frank realized they had gotten off track and said. "I'm sorry. You started to tell me how it was that Mr. Childes happened to be on board."

"Oh, yeah. Well, Mr. Childes was an early riser. He'd get here before I would, or could. Sometimes the weather isn't too nice around here, so I'd leave the cabin unlocked for him that one day of the month."

"So if he got here before you he could make himself at home, so to speak?"

"Yeah. We have an electrical cord plugged into the dock when we're tied up. It's for keeping the batteries charged up and various other uses. Mr. Childes would usually be here early enough to turn a heater on and make the coffee, which is somethin' I normally do. We keep coffee ready for our passengers, then when he'd finished whatever he was going to do, he'd catch a quick nap on the bench over there."

"Would there have been anyone else on board that morning?"

"Not much chance of it that early."

"Who goes out to the island? Are there a lot of people who go out there?"

"No. Mostly just homeowners or their guests. Sometimes we might get a tourist or two, but not very often."

"Why's that? I mean, very few tourists."

"Because, when they get out to the island there isn't much to do, except to walk around until the ferry gets back out there again to bring them back. Pretty boring for most folks."

OFFICE

"So, any thing special about the guy they pulled out'ta the drink Saturday?" Jim asked as Frank sat down at the desk across from him. He put his coffee cup down while he looked over at his partner.

"Seems pretty cut and dried, according to the coroner."

"And to you?"

"Well, I drove out to the marina and talked with the ferry skipper. Nothing seems to be out of order on that end either. Except for some missing steps." Then he added, "I talked to the two uniforms who were on the scene initially, and one of them put an attaché case belonging to a Mr. Childes in the evidence locker, should anyone ask."

"You have a look at it?"

"Yeah."

"Anything of interest?"

"Not much in it. At least nothing that seemed out of the ordinary. A couple of old business cards, some travel brochures, couple of pens, a note book with some notes about past business meetings, and a small, well worn and well read chess book"

"You gonna file the case away as an accidental death then?"

"Yeah, I s'pose so. I thought about having his car impounded but I don't really have a reason for doing so. It was in the tow lot, so I had a quick look at it. Didn't see anything out of the ordinary." Then, Frank thought about it for a few seconds, and said, "I think for the time being I'll just keep the file in my desk. I'll file it later."

Jim went back to a file he was reviewing. He admired Frank's ability to solve cases. Jim wasn't sure if Frank was just lucky, or just followed his hunches. It seemed to Jim that Frank often overlooked obvious items, yet instinctively knew when something was wrong. After a few seconds silence he said, "You hear about Kim and Don's episode early yesterday evening?"

"No, what happened?" Frank's thoughts had been wandering. Kim Larson and Don Olson were the two fellow detectives he and Jim shared this office with.

Jim looked back at Frank as he said, "Seems they were in the parking lot of that big supermarket down on the main drag going north out of town. They were doing a take down of some dealers. They had two cars set up, and when they arrived, they signaled the dealers to park in between them. The three guys in the car thought that Kim and Don were buying big this time and had agreed to show up with a huge pile of dope. All this was taking place in the center of the parking lot of the store." Jim hesitated for a moment thinking about the sequence of events as they had been explained to him.

Frank now piqued, said, "And?" Frank knew Don and Kim had bought dope in small amounts from dealers before to earn their trust, so that they could set up a proper bust.

34

"Oh. . . .Ah yeah. Well, anyway, all hell started to break loose. They had started to make the arrests. Don had the bunch covered from the front of the car, and Kim had started around the back of the dealer's car, so he could start taking them out of the car one at a time. When suddenly a car with an older man and woman came driving down the parking lot aisle heading right for him."

Frank interrupted, "They run into him?"

Jim laughed and said, "No. About the time he saw the folks in the car they'd seen him. But he was in the process of pulling his Uzi out from under his coat and the folks in the car saw it in his hand. He said their eyes bugged out, and the man jerked to a stop and backed his car up a whole lot quicker than he'd driven into where they were. After that everything went smooth."

"This the big case they've been working on for some time?"

"Yeah. I think they've got about thirty-eight more arrests to make concerning this group."

The Knight moves to attack

R	N	B	Q	K	B	N	R
P	P	P	P	P	P	P	P
			$\mathcal{P}$				
				$\mathcal{N}$			
$\mathcal{P}$	$\mathcal{P}$	$\mathcal{P}$	$\mathcal{P}$		$\mathcal{P}$	$\mathcal{P}$	$\mathcal{P}$
$\mathcal{R}$	$\mathcal{N}$	$\mathcal{B}$	$\mathcal{Q}$	$\mathcal{K}$	$\mathcal{B}$		$\mathcal{R}$

N-KB3

THIRD MONDAY IN SEPTEMBER

Frank was up early. Not because his alarm clock went off, but because he just woke up and then found he couldn't get back to sleep. Finally he got up and took his morning shower and shaved. As he traced lines through the thick shaving cream with his double-edged razor, he reflected back to when he'd started shaving.

He'd only been fifteen or so when his father told him he needed a shave. He'd been proud to think he actually needed a shave at that young age. That same afternoon his father had taken him to get his first shaving mug and razor. Now, his need to shave his daily growth of a heavy dark beard, seemed a constant ongoing chore. Tilting his head to shave up under his chin, he thought, *'Should never have started shaving that young.'* He rinsed his face in warm water, dried it, then he returned to the bedroom where he got dressed.

As he finished buttoning the last two top buttons on his shirt, he headed into his small kitchen. Frank shoved some of the dirty dishes in the kitchen sink out of the way just to make some room. He attempted to push the coffee pot under the spigot, but the pot wouldn't fit entirely under the spigot upright. Yet, he was able to get the water he needed to make a pot of coffee.

While he waited for the coffee, he went out to the hallway, and picked up his morning paper from the old hardwood oak floor. Its oak planking had been kept alive with diligent care, but the wood was dark with age. Inside his apartment, he sat at his kitchen table. The table barely fit in the kitchen, and there was only room for two chairs. He could use another chair on the outer edge, but not without blocking the doorway.

He was working on his second cup of coffee when he got to the personals column. The usual ads were present, and nothing caught his eye until he got down to the bottom of the column. There was another one of those chess moves listed. "N-KB3" He muttered to himself, "Knight to King's Bishop three. What gives?" Being a chess player himself, he tried to visualize in his mind the way the chessboard would look.

He sipped the last of his coffee from the cup, got up and added the cup to those dishes already in the sink. "Damn, guess I'd better do something about these dishes." He turned, and left the room knowing full well they would still be there when he got home.

OFFICE

As usual, Frank had gotten into the office early. Sitting in his chair relaxing, he was leaning back with his legs up and over the corner edge of his desk. His jacket, which he'd hung on the back of his chair, had a sleeve nearly touching the floor. He was reading through a few reports when Duty Sergeant, Michael Brown came into his office.

"Here's a few cases that came in Saturday on Cary Ann's computer printout. It was left on my desk instead of makin' it in here." They both knew Cary Ann, who normally took care of printing the reports during the week, had assigned one of her new office secretaries the task of printing the weekend reports and then distributing them to the various departments.

"What are they?" Frank asked. Not really interested, but knowing he would have to read through them sometime.

"Only one might interest you guys. Some guy fell off a cliff."

Frank took the computer printout from Mike. He let the sheets fan down into his lap while he held the top of the first sheet. Reading the reports, they gave him some of the basic details of the cases which he scanned quickly, then he set the files on the top of his desk. There was a copy of the coroner's report with the file. He'd let Jim read the reports as well. There was only one report on the list they would have to check into.

He reached down and slightly around to his right and pulled his notebook from the jacket pocket. His new notes were quickly added to those he had collected over the years. This new one was right after the one about, Harold Childes

*Marty Hanson, Caucasian / Male
Body was found by neighbor while walking on the beach below Mr. Hanson's property. It appeared as though he'd fallen off the top of the bluff at the back of his home. His head struck a sharp rock on the beach. Appears to be an accidental death, cause of death, cranial intrusion.*

Later in the morning, when Frank wandered into the coffee shop, he saw Cary Ann sitting alone at a table by the window. Pouring himself a cup of coffee, he moved to her side saying, "Mind if I join you?" His heart rate picking up some as he looked down at her.

"Not at all," she said, looking up. She began moving some of the morning reports she had been sorting through and dividing into groups. By moving them out of the way, he would have room for his coffee cup on the tabletop. "What are you up to today?"

She still smelled good to him. There was a sweet smell wafting up from her, like she had just gotten out of the shower. Her dark brown hair cascaded down over her left eye. Her left hand automatically came up to her face brushing the hair away revealing the roundness of her face. Her dark eyes looked at him questioningly, and her eyes were dilating.

Frank said "You look good." Then he blushed. He always enjoyed being near her, although that didn't happen often enough to suit him.

"Thank you." She smiled. "You look good, too." She liked the fact he was blushing. It showed her a side of him she hadn't seen before.

Frank was about to ask her out for lunch when one of the new secretaries came over to them, saying, "Cary Ann, I can't get my computer to work. The screen just went blank. Could you have a look at it for me?"

Cary Ann looked at Frank sensing their conversation would have gotten more personal. "Sorry, Frank. Probably just a screen saver, but I'd better have a look." She picked up her reports and started to leave, turning back she said, "We can talk some more later, if you like."

"I'd like."

ELDERS

"Mr.Elders?" He heard her ask, as he put the telephone tightly to his ear. His hearing was going, but he was refusing to acknowledge the condition.

"Yes, it is." The woman's voice on the other end had sounded young to him.

"Mr. Elders, you don't know me, but I was driving back from shopping in Oak Harbor, and as I was crossing the bridge over Deception Pass a man flagged me down. He asked if I would call you. Apparently his car quit running and he asked if you could pick him up."

"Did you get his name?"

"No, I'm sorry I didn't. He did say he was one of your chess friends."

"Really." This confused him. Clyde wasn't expecting anyone over for a game today. Then he continued, "Where did you say he was?"

"On the south end of the bridge. You know, that tourist parking area?"

"Yes, thank you, I'll go over and get him." As he hung up, he was thinking. *'Who in the world could it be?'*

After the phone was back in its cradle, he walked to the hall closet and slipped a dark blue wind breaker off a hanger. The hanger bent slightly as he pulled on the jacket's sleeve. Then, out of habit, as he passed by the small table in the hallway, he picked up his favorite camera. *'No sense missing a good shot from the bridge if there is one.'*

42

His habit of carrying his camera over the years had provided him with some excellent photos. Most of his better shots he had enlarged, and they now adorned his walls. In the driveway he opened the car door, threw his wind breaker inside on the front seat, then laid his camera on top.

It took him a little more than twenty minutes to get to the bridge, but when he did, he saw a car he was not familiar with parked on the south east side of the roadway. Most tourists would not park here as it didn't offer much protection from the passing traffic. Pulling his car in front of the other one, he parked as close to the steep rocky bank as he could. It wasn't exceptionally chilly so he left his wind breaker on the car seat when he got out, but picked up his camera. Then he started looking for whomever it was that had been coming to see him.

He looked out toward the center of the bridge and saw a man standing there, as if looking at the view in the distance. Slipping the camera strap over his head, Clyde started toward the bridge. As he drew near the man, he recognized him. He stuck out his hand in a gesture of friendship and it was taken.

"Nice of you to come."

"Sure, no problem. Having some car trouble, huh?"

"Yes. But I don't think it's anything serious. I'll call from your place and arrange for a repair garage to tow it in, if you don't mind?"

"Not at all." Clyde was wondering, *'Why hadn't he had the woman just call a tow truck for him. Why wait for me in the first place?'*

"While I was waiting for you, I've been admiring the view from here. It's quite compelling." His manner of speech was an invitation to share the view.

"Yes, it is," Clyde said, as he turned his head to get a better look. "Hummm, it is an excellent view today," He moved close to the cement rail. "The air's nice and clear. Let me get a shot from here."

After he finished settling himself on the edge of the cement railing, he took one photo, and wound the film for the next exposure. With his finger on the button, ready for his next photo shot, he felt the physical movement of his clothing sliding across the top of the cement rail, then the rush of air around his body. His arms and legs were flailing at the air, the camera dangling below his head as he plummeted downward.

Walking away, the man felt no remorse. The man he'd just pushed meant nothing to him. The bitter remembrance of Clyde's poking fun at his error, still remained fresh in his mind.

Below the bridge, and out toward the Straight of Juan De Fuca, two men were fishing just outside of Deception Pass, and they had decided it was time to head back in toward the marina. Jasper pulled at the starter rope of the fifteen horse powered outboard motor twice before it sputtered to life. As the boat began to move slowly toward the narrow opening, they reeled their fishing lines in and stowed the fishing poles away.

When they were about a quarter of a mile away from the bridge, his fishing partner broke the silence between them, saying, "Hey, look over there." His stubby fingers pointing the way. "What's that in the water?"

Jasper turned to look, and turned the boat slightly in the same direction his partner had pointed. As they neared the object in the water, they both knew what it was. "Damn!" Jasper said. "Let's see if we can get him aboard."

It took them several minutes to get the man's body into the boat. They had to be careful so as not to tip the boat over too far while pulling the weight of the body into the boat.

Jasper's partner had taken the camera with the leather strap from around the dead man's head and neck, and laid it in the bottom of the boat. When they finished, his partner said, "We'd better get a move on, the outgoing tidal currents already starting to pick up." As it was, if they hadn't started in when they did, Clyde Elders body might never have been found.

With the outboard motor in gear they motored as fast as they could toward the marina. Both men were aware the current here could work into a fast and often dangerous situation. Their concern was that the small outboard motor they were using on this trip might not be sufficient to over ride the current's flow. They went in close to the southern rock wall of the pass, to take advantage of the counter currents there, as it helped them along. If it had not been for the tidal condition, they would have taken much longer to fish.

Once they cleared the rocky outcropping of land that separated Deception Pass and the marina, it was only minutes before they were tied up to the dock in Coronet Bay. The two of them took Clyde Elders body out of the boat and laid him on the marina's fuel dock. The Harbor Master hadn't believed them at first about finding a body, but once he had a look for himself he went back to the office and called the police.

The Bishop leaves home

R	N	B	Q	K	B	N	R
P	P	P	P	P	P	P	P
		$\mathcal{B}$		$\mathcal{P}$			
					$\mathcal{N}$		
$\mathcal{P}$	$\mathcal{P}$	$\mathcal{P}$	$\mathcal{P}$		$\mathcal{P}$	$\mathcal{P}$	$\mathcal{P}$
$\mathcal{R}$	$\mathcal{N}$	$\mathcal{B}$	$\mathcal{Q}$	$\mathcal{K}$			$\mathcal{R}$

B-QB4

47

FIRST MONDAY OF OCTOBER

Frank hadn't slept well the night before, and when his alarm went off he hesitated getting up. He lay there in the warmth of his bed covers feeling the comfort as long as he dared to procrastinate. He knew he would fall asleep again if he didn't get a move on. Groggily, he got up and still naked, headed for the kitchen. Once he had the coffee started, he took his morning shower in hotter water than normal to ward off the chill of the morning air. This resulted in having to wipe the fogged mirror while shaving, so he could see the reflection of his face. He was thinking 'Men's beards should stop growing when they reached the age where it would equal a woman's menopause.' As usual, he maneuvered the razor around the cleft in his chin.

He heard it gurgling from the bedroom, and had just gotten to the coffeepot before it started to boil over. Turning the coffee off, he went back to the bedroom where he finished dressing. Minutes later, Frank went to retrieve his morning paper from the hallway, glancing at his watch on the way. Now at his kitchen table he was drinking coffee much stronger than he would have liked. It had boiled longer than it should have, and he was paying the price. As he read through the personals column, he came across the last item in the column which was, "3 B-QB4."

He pondered the chess move and decided that when he got home that night he would set up his chess board and play this latest move, Bishop to Queen's Bishop four. He would also play the other moves, to see what the board looked like with the chess moves visibly placed on it. His curiosity had driven him to make a list of the previous moves. The list was attached to the front of his refrigerator with a miniature milk bottle magnet. He was aware this would show only one of the chess players moves on the board, and he knew he would have to guess at what chess moves that the person who played the black pieces would have made in the game.

He finished his coffee and ate a small bowl of cold cereal with a banana sliced on it. He washed his morning dishes, letting them drain dry in the dish rack on the drain board next to the sink. Looking at the two remaining bananas laying on a paper sack near the toaster, he picked them up and turned them over in his hand. The brown freckles from two days before had now gotten much larger and he dropped the bananas into the garbage under the sink. He figured they were still good, but he also knew from habit, he wouldn't eat them unless they were a fresh yellow color.

He got his jacket out of the closet, combed his hair again, noting the strands of gray at the temples, then he left for the office.

OFFICE

Jim and Frank were talking about one of the parolees who hadn't been in to see his parole officer for two of his last scheduled appointments. Between them they decided that Jim would go out to the parolee's supposed residence and have a talk with him. He would have to explain why he wasn't complying with the rules set forth in his release stipulations. Normally this would be one of the parole officer's duties, but that department was swamped, and Jim had volunteered his help.

As they were speaking about the parolee, Sergeant Brown came into their office and handed Jim the computer printout for the weekend activity, saying, "Here's the latest and greatest, fella's."

"Anything exciting goin' on?"

"Nope. Not much anyway. There was another accident though. This one happened on Whidbey Island, and there was a hit and run downtown last night but they caught the driver shortly after he'd driven away from the scene."

Something about the accidental death bothered Frank. His mind kicked into gear. 'Kinda strange about all these accidental deaths starting to happen, or are they accidental?' His curiosity was being kindled as he added another death entry into his notebook.

Clyde Elders, Caucasian / Male,
Apparently fell while taking photographs
from the Deception Pass bridge linking
Whidbey Island with the mainland.
Camera found around victim's neck is in
evidence locker. Appears to be an
accidental death, cause of death,
drowning.

The uniformed officer's names who were at the scene, were listed on the back of the form, as well as the names and addresses of the two fishermen.

Curious, Frank wondered if these recent cases were related somehow. He put the report down on his desk and thumbed through his Rolodex for the phone number of the Whidbey Island police department. When he found the number he was looking for he dialed the phone number and waited while it rang.

"Whidbey Island Police Department. How can I help you?" A strong male voice had answered.

"Yes, this is Frank Chambers of The Everett police department. Can I speak to one of your detectives on duty?"

"Sure, hang on."

A couple of minutes later he heard, "Mr. Chambers, Bob Powers here. How can I help you?"

"Actually Bob I don't have anything but curiosity at the moment. I'm curious if you found anything suspicious about the accident involving a Mr.Clyde Elders? He's the guy who fell of the bridge up there."

"Ah...Mr. Elders. No, not that I could find. Seems like any other accident, course we haven' finished looking into it yet." It seemed odd to Bob for a detective on the mainland to be calling about a case up here. Bob continued, "Just curious you say?"

"Yeah. I've had a couple of accidental deaths down here lately, and you had another one up there as well. I'm sorry to bother you about this Bob, it's just a feeling is all."

"Accidents happen all the time though."

"Yeah. I know. Would you mind if I talk to the fishermen who found him?"

"Not at all. Hang on I'll get the phone numbers for you." Frank could hear the rustling of paper in the background. When he came back to the telephone, he said, "I've only got one number here. Apparently one of them didn't have a phone."

After Frank wrote the number down he said, "Thanks Bob."

"No problem. If you turn something up, you'll keep in touch, right?"

"Like I said, Bob, it's just a curiosity at this point in time."

After Frank finished talking with Bob Powers, he pushed the off button on the phone, then pushed in the telephone number he'd been given. A woman answered on the third ring with a cheerful, "Hello."

"Mrs. Jasper?" Frank asked.

"Who's calling please?"

"Mrs. Jasper, I'm Frank Chambers from the Sheriff's Office. Is Mr. Jasper home this morning?"

"No," she said hesitantly. "He isn't, he's at work."

"Where would that be?"

"He's a machinist at the Navy Base." A chill began to run up her back.

"The Naval Air Base on the island there?"

"Yes."

"Thank you, Mrs. Jasper."

"Anything I can help you with?" She said.

"No. Nothing to be alarmed about, but thank you."

When he hung up the phone, he said to Jim, "Jim I'm gonna go out to the Navy Air Base on Whidbey Island to talk to one of the fishermen who found this latest guy's body."

"Okay, Pardner. I'll go check on our gent that doesn't seem to think he needs to check in with his parole officer."

Frank stopped before he left the office, turned toward Jim saying, "You know you could ask Kim and Don to stop by his place during their night shift. That way he wouldn't be expecting anyone at an early morning hour."

"Something to think about all right." They often had Don Olson and Kim Larson, the other two detectives who shared their office, look into things for them at strange hours of the night during their shift. They in turn did things for Kim and Don during the daylight hours that they couldn't do without interrupting their sleep time.

ANGER

He'd humiliated himself enough with the huge error he'd made in the game, and he was angry because of the mistake. "Damn them! They shouldn't have laughed at me!"

Most of them hadn't laughed out loud, at least not in his presence, but one player had snickered openly at his mistake. Even after the evening was over, they had talked behind his back. One man he hadn't expected to find humor in his loss, did.

Part of the anger he felt toward this one man, was because he had been an investor in one of his own real estate deals in the past. He knew it shouldn't bother him but it did. He had needed someone to introduce him into this group, and he had used this man for his connections to get into the game. He knew it wouldn't have been possible to arrange an introduction to this group without this one man's approval. Even he didn't fully understand his contempt for this man, but it was there none the less.

After the final match game was over, he had tried to pass the error off as an honest mistake, which it had been. He himself had said things to those around him, like, "Well, it happens that way sometimes," or " Easy come easy go." But the outcome had been very crucial to his personal well being. He'd poured his very heart and soul into the competition. Not to mention the fact that it had cost him money he couldn't really afford to spend.

His business was at an all time low now. This latest gamble he'd made by purchasing the large tract of land on the edge of the lake where he had planned to harvest most of the trees for his only real profit in the venture. The speculation homes that were to be built were of a marginal profit at best. Then he'd been dealt a defeating blow by the local city commissioners. They had reversed their decision as to his being able to cut the trees. They were against his plan which, in their mind, would almost leave the tract of land devoid of foliage.

It hadn't been planned to cut all the trees down. He didn't tell them he was going to cut a large share of them, especially the largest ones. He had tried to assure them he wasn't going to leave the land without plant life, but he'd been unsuccessful in his quest to convince the commissioners.

He had been in desperate need of the chess game prize money for his business to survive. Now it had been taken from his grasp by one quick unthinking movement. It was gone....just gone. In that one split second his economic futures had disappeared and these people here with him now in these opulent surroundings, weren't even sympathetic. But how could they be, they didn't know of his circumstances. He'd covered his tracks well. He'd been successful in making them think he was well off financially. It was their finding humor in his chess match downfall that made him angry.

'They will never laugh at me again!'

U.S. NAVY

Frank stopped at the main gate at the Naval Air Base and was approached by a uniformed guard. As he showed his identification, he told the guard he was here to speak to someone about a case he was presently working on. The guard had asked, "Are you here about any military personnel, Sir?"

"No, I'm not. I only need to speak to a person who works here on the base and has some knowledge about an accident that happened recently."

"Civilian personnel, then, Sir?"

"Yes."

"Very well, Sir."

Frank was then given directions to the civilian personnel office. The guard at the gate said, "You drive straight ahead sir, until you come to "Glouchester St." Turn right and the civilian personnel building will be the first building on your right." Then the guard waved him on through and into the interior of the military base.

He drove the short block and parked in the small, nearly empty parking lot. He could see the gate he'd just come through and wondered why the guard hadn't just pointed the building out to him. Frank followed the path others had made across the divider covered in small shrubs and smiled when he thought of how landscape architects put these dividers in, but they never leave a regular pathway through them.

When he got to the building covered in white siding, he walked up the four low wooden steps, then across the wooden deck, and entered through the metal door. Inside, the brightness from the neon lighting struck him. There was a chest high counter running the width of the entry area. Once at the counter, a young woman who appeared to be much too thin to be healthy, rose from her desk nearby and came toward him. The heels of her shoes clattered on the floor and sounded like someone much heavier.

"May I be of help?"

"Yes please." Frank pulled his departmental identification wallet from his inside jacket pocket. He opened it for the young lady's inspection and said, "I need to talk with one of your civilian employees. A man by the name of Mr. Jasper. He's a machinist here on the base."

She looked a little disturbed, or bewildered, he couldn't be sure which, and said, "Just a moment please." She walked to the rear of the room to a desk where an older woman was busy working. The other woman looked up as she was being told about Frank and what he wanted. She got up from her desk and came to the counter.

"You're a police officer?"

"Yes, Ma'am. Detective Frank Chambers." He held his badge and identification picture out for her to see.

"The man you want to see, is he in some kind of trouble with the law?"

58

It never surprised Frank anymore. It seemed that whenever he asked to speak to someone like this, that whoever he was talking with almost always thought the person he was asking about was guilty of something.

"Oh, no Ma'am. It's just that I'd like to ask him about an accident he may have witnessed. He might have some information about a case I'm working on. There's no problem with Mr. Jasper."

"Very well. I'll locate him for you." She had said it in such a huffy manner that it left Frank feeling a little upset with her attitude. He was well aware that if he wanted to exercise some authority, she would find Mr. Jasper for him no matter what she may have thought. However he was on a military base and the rules were different here.

She walked over to a computer terminal, pushed a key then hit the enter key, which brought up a personnel search menu. It was only a few seconds before she had the information he needed. She then returned to the counter where Frank was waiting and instructed him on how to find the building where Mr. Jasper worked.

Frank had to wind his way around a few buildings to find the one he was searching for. When Frank arrived at his destination he was met just inside the entry door by a portly man whose shirt was trying to escape from the top of his pants and the bottom button of the shirt had pulled apart leaving a gap that exposed the man's undershirt. He was wearing a name and identity badge that indicated he was a plant supervisor.

"Mr. Chambers?"

"Yes."

"The personnel office called me and told me to expect you. I have Mr. Jasper waiting in my office for you."

"Thanks." Frank then followed him around the corner of the wall they were standing next to and into an office which had more desks crowded into it than one would normally find in this much space. There was only one person inside. In the office Frank reached out his hand and it Mr. Jasper took it. They shook hands and Mr. Jasper looked a little tense. His thin black hair had been swept back by his hand, and beads of perspiration now adorned his forehead. Frank turned around to face the supervisor, who smiled, understanding what was expected of him. Then he turned and left the room.

Turning back around, Frank said, "I'm Frank Chambers with the Sheriff's Office. I hope you don't mind the intrusion while you're at work but I need to follow up on some things while they're still fresh in your mind. I'm here to ask you about the body you found in the water outside of Deception Pass a few days ago."

"Oh, okay."

Frank could see him start to relax, and he sat down in a nearby chair. Frank did so as well. He gave Mr. Jasper a few moments, then Frank started by asking. "Notice anything unusual about the body when you found it?"

"Nope, not a thing that I noticed. Except for the camera around his neck. But when you're fishing a dead body out of the water, that's unusual enough."

Frank could understand the man's feelings and continued saying, "Any idea where he came from?"

"Yeah. Well, maybe. I'm pretty sure he was one'a the two guys we saw on the bridge earlier."

"You noticed two people on the bridge before finding the body?"

"Well I saw that there were two guys on the bridge. I just figured they were together. Couldn't really tell from where we were fishin', and we didn't watch 'em. I just saw the two of 'em once when we turned around to troll back towards the bridge. Then we turned back seaward after awhile."

"Did you see him fall?"

"No sir."

"Was the other person, or anyone else still on the bridge afterwards?"

"Don't think so. Least ways I don't remember seein' anyone else after that."

"Were you and your fishing partner drinking during the day?"

"Well, we had a few beers while we were out there but we weren't drunk or anything."

"Was the water rough that day?"

"No. The tide was just changing, so it was pretty quiet. No overfalls or wave action at all. Just the beginning of the outgoing current."

"You wear glasses?"

"Nope. Don't need 'em."

Frank asked a few more routine questions about the time of day, about how long it took them to get to the body, and what they did after they had the body in their boat and one or two other things.

Satisfied with the answers he'd gotten, he finished with, "Well, thank you for your help in this matter, Mr. Jasper."

"No problem."

On the way out of the building Frank was met again by the supervisor. "Any problems with Jasper?"

"No, he was very helpful." Then after a moment Frank added, "Too bad we don't have more good folks like him."

"Ohh .... ahh .... Good."

QUINE

The afternoon weather could be seen building up in the distance. Yet Jacques Quine believed he still had time for a safe flight up to Nanaimo, British Columbia, though he had to leave before the weather ceiling set down in this area preventing his flight. He was expected, as it had been planned for him to have Sunday dinner with his daughter and her husband. He'd been spending the last few days with some old friends in Seattle. Jacques hadn't seen some of them since his wife passed away nearly seven years before.

Jacques and his friends were walking slowly down the tilted ramp to the floating dock where his plane waited. As they talked, he caught a glimpse of his plane bobbing in the wake of a passing boat. Just as one small wavelet rolled his plane gently toward him at a slight angle, his vision caught sight of something. Before his mind could register the thought in his mind, his attention was whisked away by a comment from one of his friends. His mind reverted back to the conversation, the other thought now gone.

While Jacques and his friends were standing on the float plane dock saying their good-byes, the dock attendant, who had been waiting patiently, wanted to hurry things along because he had other things he had to get done. He came up to Jacques' side and mentioned, "Mr. Quine your mechanic was here yesterday and he said everything checked out fine."

Jacques stopped speaking, turned to the dock attendant saying, "My mechanic? I don't have a mechanic here." Jacques was as mystified about it as the dock attendant.

"Oh. Well, maybe I made a mistake. I thought he was here looking at your plane, but maybe it was one of the charter planes that was in here yesterday."

The interruption had brought him to break up the conversation, and he quickly finished saying his good-byes, and climbed into the pilot's seat of his plane. His friends were still standing on the dock waving goodbye as he started the radial engine for its warm up, the big three bladed propeller whop, whopping through the still air. Jacques scanned the various dials on the aircraft's instrument panel in front of him, but did not notice the two very small wires pressed back into the recess along the semi vertical windshield and wing support to his left.

He watched the oil pressure gauge needle rise until the oil pressure was at a satisfactory level and the fuel gauge showed a full tank. He checked his controls and everything seemed fine. Satisfied, he pulled his shoulder harness down and snapped it into place, then signaled the dock attendant to release his tie downs to be cast loose. Ready at last he waved a final farewell to his friends and slowly taxied the plane away from the floating dock, turning it toward Ballard Locks.

He was aware of the slight cross wind out on the lake and adjusted his trim tabs for it. When the area ahead of his path was clear of all boating traffic, he shoved his engine throttle to full power for the take off. When he did this, a small micro switch that was taped to a piece of support metal under the panel activated a small timer that had also been taped near the micro switch.

The large radial engine began to pull the high wing monoplane rapidly across the rippled surface of the lake sending sprays of water out from both floats. Soon the plane's floats were up on their steps, then they lifted free of the water's surface. The wind swept the last of the remaining water off the surface of the floats and left it trailing behind. After the plane reached a comfortable air speed, Jacques eased the throttle back to the cruising speed setting. The small timer had now been running just seconds over four minutes.

The skies were starting to darken from the cloud front closing in on his present location. A small rain squall was becoming apparent to him just to the south west of his position, but he didn't think much of it, or the possible wind in front of it as it would not pose a problem for his flight. He would rapidly outrun it. He straightened his plane out heading slightly west of north, and almost straight toward Lopez Island, the Puget Sound shipping channel now directly under him.

Eight minutes into the flight, there was a small puff of smoke above the Port wing, quickly lost in the slip stream. The plastique explosive charge and its detonator had been covered with silver colored duct tape, blending in with the shiny aluminum surface to disguise it being there. The explosive effect was able to shear the joint where the wing was attached to the plane's fuselage. The weakened wing peeled away, falling seaward as the plane plunged to its left, and the starboard wing was high in the air. Then the plane started a radical spiraling dive down, the large radial engine whining loudly as it aimed at the darkness of the waters of Puget Sound. Only Jacques could hear his voice saying "Oh, my God!" He knew there was no way to control his fate.

The Queen's Pawn Steps Forward

R	N	B	Q	K	B	N	R
P	P	P	P	P	P	P	P
		$\mathcal{B}$		$\mathcal{P}$			
			$\mathcal{P}$		$\mathcal{N}$		
$\mathcal{P}$	$\mathcal{P}$	$\mathcal{P}$			$\mathcal{P}$	$\mathcal{P}$	$\mathcal{P}$
$\mathcal{R}$	$\mathcal{N}$	$\mathcal{B}$	$\mathcal{Q}$	$\mathcal{K}$			$\mathcal{R}$

P-Q3

66

THIRD MONDAY OF OCTOBER
Frank found another new chess move in his morning
paper. Lately he had made it a habit to look through
the personals column first every day, then he would
read the rest of the paper afterwards. This morning the
chess move was "P-Q3" "Ahh," he said to no one but
himself. "Pawn to Queen three." His curiosity had
taken over and he immediately got up from his table,
went to his hall closet, and reached up to get his chess
set off the shelf.

Back in the kitchen, he put the board on the table and
began sorting the chess pieces so he could set them
up on the chessboard. He looked at his list of moves,
and made the moves for the white pieces as he had
seen them appear in the paper. Finishing the moves,
he put the list of chess moves along side the chess
board.

WHITE	BLACK
1 P-K4	1 ??
2 N-KB3	2 ??
3 B-QB4	3 ??
4 P-Q3	4 ??

He assumed the moves were for the white pieces.
Because in chess games, it is customary for the white
pieces to move first. However, there hadn't been any
countering chess moves appear in the paper and this
was making him curious. How can you play chess if no
one plays against you? It seemed like a mystery game
with only one side making moves. He tried to mentally
fill in the moves for the black pieces but nothing made
any sense to him. He needed to make moves that
would fit in with the white chess moves that had
already been made.

Later in the morning when he'd arrived in his office at slightly past eight, he almost expected to find a computer print out lying on his desk....a computer printout containing another accidental death over the week end. It seemed to him that recently every time one of these chess moves appeared in the newspaper, someone had died under what seemed to be accidental circumstances.

"Afternoon, Frank," Jim said in jest. For once Frank was actually late.

Frank knew why Jim was kidding him and followed with, "Hey, I'm only a few minutes late."

"Yes, I know. It's just that you're usually the one that's here on time or even early."

"Why are you here early?"

"Well, Janet and I had another argument this morning so I left early."

"Anything serious?"

"I hope not. I just tried to politely mention that she needed to clean up our apartment."

Frank knew Jim was almost a neatness freak, not quite but almost. Frank had been to Jim and Janet's apartment recently and it had been a mess. It had been Jim's apartment but he had convinced his girl friend to move in with him.

"She's got a pretty heavy work schedule doesn't she?"

68

"Not anymore. She's been downsized. So now she's home all the time. Of course she is looking for another position, but while she's home she should have time to clean up our place."

Frank didn't like domestic squabbles, especially with personal friends. He wanted to change the subject so he asked, "Anything going on this morning?"

"Not much different from any other time . . . You?"

"Naw." Then Frank added, "Find your errant parolee, Joey?"

"Nope. I checked out the address his parole officer gave me, but he wasn't around. Seems he hasn't been seen by any neighbors lately either."

"Gonna follow it up?"

"Well it's not a top priority, but I'll pursue it when I can. Who knows he might come in on his own yet."

Later while he was on his way back from a coffee break, Frank passed Sergeant Brown's desk. "Morning, Mike."

"Morning, Frank." The sergeant said without looking up from the newspaper he was reading.

"I almost expected to find a computer printout on my desk this morning when I came in."

"Why's that?" He said, now looking up at Frank as if he'd forgotten to do something.

"Well, recently, on every other Monday, that is, you've given me a computer printout that had an accidental death that happened over the week end."

"Disappointed you didn't have one this morning?" He was relieved to know he hadn't forgotten to do something.

"No. It's just that there was a chess move in the paper this morning." After he'd said it, he knew it had come out wrong and that it wouldn't be understood.

"Chess move?" Mike had looked up at him like he was nuts when he had said that.

"Oh, nothin, I guess." He knew it sounded weird, even to him, but it still seemed strange to him.

Then, just as he started to turn away, he heard Mike say, "Course there is that plane that went down somewhere in the Sound over the weekend."

"Plane?" He hadn't heard about any airplane having disappeared.

"Yeah, it was on the news last night but they haven't found any debris or wreckage as far as I know yet."

"Commercial or private plane."

"Private plane."

Back in his office Frank picked up the phone and dialed a memorized phone number. Fortunately one of his neighbors worked in the news department at one of the local television stations.

In the distance he heard, "News desk."

"Joanne, Frank Chambers here."

"What's up, Frank?"

"I'm hoping you can tell me."

"About what?"

"I understand there was an airplane lost this weekend, somewhere in the Puget Sound area."

"Yes, there was. Hang on a sec okay?" . . . Frank heard papers being moved about in her search of her desk top. Then she was back, "A Mr. Jacques Quine left Lake Union Saturday in his float plane, but never arrived at his destination. Seems a sail boat, which was out on the water for a day sail, said that on their way back in toward Shilshole Marina they heard an engine running at high RPMs just before something hit the water somewhere behind them. They called the Coast Guard who took the report. The area was searched briefly, but to no avail."

"You got any idea where the pilot was going?"

"Yes. Umm, let's see . . . Ahh, here it is. According to some friends he was on his way to visit his daughter and her husband in Nanaimo, B.C. He was supposed to be there for dinner yesterday, Sunday."

"Got anything on the daughter?"

"Umm, yeah, her name's Lisa Bradshaw. Apparently she lives on a boat in one of the marinas up there."

"Thanks, Joanne."

"You betcha. You owe me."

CHIEF'S CALL

The duty sergeant caught Frank as he was coming in through the door reserved for police personnel. "Frank the chief wants to see you as soon as you're able this morning."

"Okay, thanks." Frank hurried to his office and called the chief's office. "You wanted to see me, sir?"

"Yeah, Frank. You got time now?"

"Yessir. I'll be right down."

When Frank walked into the chief's office, the chief said. "Close the door, Frank." Now Frank was worried.

After Frank closed the door and sat down, the chief turned to face him saying, "Frank, I got a call from the police chief on Whidbey Island. They were asking me why you seemed interested in a couple of accidental deaths that had taken place over there."

Frank knew this wasn't a statement, but a question. "Yessir. The problem is I don't actually have much to go on. It's just a curiosity so far."

"Listen, Frank, you're a good detective but you should let me in on these things. You pretty much have free rein, but I'd like to be kept abreast of things."

"Yessir. I'm in the process of gathering some information that I'll present to you when I'm more comfortable with it."

"Okay, let me see what you have when it's ready."

"I'll do that."

"Are there any other areas I might get calls from?"

"Not yet, sir."

"Good. That's all I've got, Frank." As Frank started to leave, he added, "One more thing. If I get any more calls like this, I'll tell them the same thing I told the chief at Whidbey Island. That you're working on an ongoing investigation."

Frank smiled. "Thanks chief. I'll keep you up to speed on what I find. If anything."

That afternoon Frank got a phone call from Bob Powers on the Whidbey Island police department. "Frank we had the film developed that was found in this guy Clyde Elder's camera. I had a couple of extra prints made and I'll send them over to you."

"Thanks, Bob. I appreciate your help and the prints."

NANAIMO

Frank made a point to stop by the chief's office and fill him in on his curiosity and his theory about the ongoing chess game and its moves. Also, that he thought there might be some kind of a connection between the accidental deaths taking place. After the discussion was nearly ended, Frank said, "So, I'd like to take a car from the motor pool over to Vancouver Island."

"Uuummm. Can't let you take a state vehicle over there, Frank. You may be onto something, but to take one of our police vehicles over there, don't think so."

"Okay, what if I take my own car over to Vancouver?"

"I've no problem with that. Tell you what, keep track of your expenses and mileage. Maybe later I can get you reimbursed."

"Works for me, Chief." Frank was just glad to get the okay to go ahead.

The next morning Frank caught the early ferry from Port Angeles across the Juan De Fuca Straight to Victoria, British Columbia. The trip across had been easy and comfortable, because the morning wind hadn't started blowing against the resisting tidal currents. After the ferry had docked in Victoria, Frank cleared customs then, as a professional courtesy, he informed the Royal Canadian Mounted Police of his intentions while he was on the island. Informing them he was there only to seek some information. They were only concerned whether he was carrying a firearm. When they established that he was not armed, they wished him good luck in his quest.

75

After Frank drove the hour or so to Nanaimo, he decided to stop for a late breakfast before he went to see the Bradshaws. Parking on a side street, he found the pavement still damp from a light rain. He was only a block or so from the Public Marina, an area he enjoyed coming to on occasion for lunch, as this was where he and his first wife Miriam used to come. The two of them would watch the boats come and go, as well as the many tourists who milled around.

Sometimes, even yet, he would catch the small ferry across to Newcastle Island where he'd spend the day exploring the small island. "I got'ta bring Cary over here sometime."

He thought, "It'd be a good place for an intimate picnic on a warm day."

Across the street from where he parked the car, he saw the sign for the small hole-in-the-wall café. He pushed the door open and when he entered, he saw the magazine rack filled with a variety of old and new magazines. These were apparently for those who had to wait for their meal. No one greeted him so, hesitantly, he moved to his right into the close dining area.

A young lady with a French accent seemed to pop up out of nowhere, greeted him and asked, "Can I be of help?" Frank had to listen carefully to understand her.

"Yes, I'd like to get some breakfast."

She pointed to a small table nearby, its top cluttered with various items such as salt and pepper, jam, syrup, an ashtray, ketchup and the like. He walked to where she had pointed, and sat down. His eyes searched through the items on the table, but he didn't see a menu. Just as he was about to ask for one, a voice of another woman behind a chest high wall to his right asked, "How do you want your eggs?"

Surprised at not having a choice for his breakfast, he said, "Over medium."

"Bacon or ham?"

"Bacon."

"Coffee or tea."

"Coffee."

It didn't take long before his breakfast was placed on the table for him. It consisted of coffee, four slices of toast and jam, several strips of bacon, two eggs over medium, fresh fruit, orange juice and the French girl standing along side asking if he'd like anything else.

When he said, "No," she sat across from him while she continued talking with him in a general conversation as he ate. It reminded him of being home with his family where there was always some conversation going on while a home cooked meal was being eaten. The meal was very good, the company delightful and the cost seemed low. He'd enjoyed the meal and the company so much he forgot to get a receipt to put with his trip expense report.

Frank found a phone booth and a phone book nearby. He punched the numbers on the telephone, and after answering, the Bradshaws gave him directions to their boat. He drove slowly, winding around a few streets near the water front, finally finding the place he was looking for and parked in the lot at the Market Place mall.

As Frank walked down the wooden walkway alongside the Pub, he saw a man about his own age, or perhaps a little younger, waiting for him on the walkway ahead.

"Mr. Chambers, Eh?" the man said.

"That's right. You Mr. Bradshaw?"

"At's roight." Some Scottish brogue seemed apparent to Frank.

Frank followed him down a narrow side dock until they reached a large ketch-rigged sailboat. The sails were covered with sail covers to protect them from the sunlight when it made appearances, the spruce masts above sparkled through several coats of varnish. The sides of the main cabin gleamed, matching the appearance of the spruce masts.

They stepped aboard through the boarding gate in the safety lines, walked aft, stepped down into the cockpit and climbed down the five steps into the main salon of the boat. Its interior bulkheads were dark from the color of fine teak woods. A bright nautical lamp on the main salon table lit up the interior. It was a feeling of instant comfort. He could easily understand the reason for people living this way on boats. After the introductions were made, Frank was offered, and accepted, a cup of tea. It was stronger than he expected it to be. A small plate of cookies was also placed on the table for him.

After some small talk about boats and their lifestyle Frank said, "I'm sorry to bother you folks at a time like this, but I do appreciate your seeing me."

"It's about my father, isn't it?" Lisa Bradshaw asked.

"Well, yes and no." She looked at him curiously, then he continued. " Actually I'm not sure what I'm looking for. I am curious about your father's intended flight up here."

Not knowing where to start, she simply said, "He was coming up for dinner with us on Sunday. We didn't get to see daddy very often. In fact he hasn't been up here since last year when he was up for the big game."

"When he came up, did he fly up each time?"

"Yes. He's been a pilot for years and said it was easier to fly than to spend the time driving. He would rent a car or catch a taxi when he got where he was going if he needed one"

"Where would he leave his plane when he was here?"

"Normally at the Canadian flight dock downtown. It's just this side of the public docks."

Frank was familiar with the commercial float plane docks as he had seen them coming and going from the floating dock. He continued, "Did your father have a regular aircraft mechanic who maintained his plane?"

"Yes, but not up here in Canadian waters."

"I'd like his name and address if you have it."

"I'm sorry I don't know who that is."

He might be able to track that down, and while he made a note, he said. "Your dad was a hockey fan, I'd guess?" The thought just came out verbally, rather than just remaining quietly in his mental thought stream.

"No, not really."

"Oh. Well, you mentioned something about his being here for the big game."

"Yes, but it's a championship chess match that he wanted to play in. It's a game that's played every few years." She stopped for a few moments while she searched her mind. "I think they play it every five years."

Frank's curiosity came alive at this comment. "Chess match?" He'd recalled the fact that Mr. Hanson had a well read chess book in his attaché case.

"Yes. I think it's referred to as the Million Dollar Club."

"Holy smokes! That is a high dollar chess club. Did your father ever play in this chess game?" The thought of huge prize money for a chess game outside of international tournament play, and for just a bunch of players who got together, was a startling element for him.

"Oh, sure he did. He played every time they held the match games."

"I've never heard of this chess group," Frank said. Not that he'd heard of many chess groups.

"It's not a well known group. They only let a few very select players into the game."

"What determines who gets to play?" He was asking now more out of curiosity.

"Actually I don't know how that is determined. Generally the game is by invitation only. Also, it's usually the same fifteen or so men that play in the tournament. Except every few years they allow a new member, or two, in the group to replace someone who has left the area or passed away."

"Why do they call it the million dollar club?"

"Oh. That's because the only prize awarded for the tournament is one million dollars to the winner of the final match."

Frank sat back, his eyes widened as it registered in his mind. "My God. That's a hell of a prize!"

"Yes it is."

"Where does the million bucks come from?"

"Well, they play some elimination games to begin with. When it's narrowed down to a group of ten men who will play for the grand prize, they charge an entrance fee to get into the final game competition. I think daddie"s last entrance fee was something like one hundred, twenty five thousand American dollars to play in the tournament."

Franks mind was racing, trying to figure out in his mind what that would amount to as he made another note in his note pad and as he started doing the math. He then said, "That's a million, two hundred fifty thousand."

"Yes. Then after the million dollar purse is given to the winner of the chess match and all the expenses are paid, the referee gets whatever is left over in the fund. Even that is usually a substantial amount."

"Why would they do that for a referee?"

"To assure the referee remains impartial toward all players. Although the position is one of honor, his decisions are never questioned."

"Mrs. Bradshaw I hate to ask you this question, but are you aware of any enemies your father might have?"

She thought a few seconds, then, "I doubt it. He was old enough that any enemies he might have made in his life would be long past."

"Would you know who any of the other players in this million dollar game might be?"

"No. No, not that I can think of, however I'll let you know if I can come up with any names later."

ULMAN

Harry Ulman was fishing from the comfort of his twenty eight foot power boat. The weather was cold, but forgiving, and Harry was comfortable with the heat level of his small propane heating system on the boat. He was dressed warmly, and if he did catch a chill, he had only to go into the interior of the boat to warm up.

As it was, he left the sliding door to the inner cabin ajar, with his fishing chair near the opening where he could take advantage of the warmth coming out of the doorway. He usually fished this area, more out of fond memories than anything else. He had caught one of his largest fish ever near here. He even kidded people when he told the story saying that even the picture of the fish weighed thirty eight pounds. That had been back in the old days when there had still been a lot of fish left, and it had happened right in this area.

Harry had arrived at his favored fishing spot about a half hour earlier, and hadn't noticed the small boat in the distance that seemed to be following him. He was trolling slowly along a northwest, southeast course and the boat was on auto pilot. He had a long cord with a switch near him that was plugged into the autopilot system which allowed him the ability to change course when it was required from the back of the boat where he was sitting.

Suddenly, out of the corner of his eye, he saw someone wave at him. He waved back without thinking, then the small boat came toward him. When it was alongside, he said to the boats only passenger, "I didn't know you were a fisherman."

"Well, I'm not an avid fisherman like yourself but I do like getting out on the water occasionally. However, I have to admit it's cooler this morning that I had expected it to be." He had spent a great deal of time on the water in boats but he could count on one hand the amount of times he had been fishing in his life and would have several fingers left over.

Harry, aware of his own comforts and seeing the gloves on the other man's hands asked, "Would you like to come aboard to warm up. I've plenty of room."

"Uhh, well sure, but what about my boat?" He had planned on being invited aboard. Getting the invitation had been easier than he thought.

"We'll just tie it off on the starboard stern cleat. It'll be okay there."

Harry helped his guest aboard, reached into a nearby locker and got out another deck chair, unfolded it, and put it down on the deck nearby for his guest, and they sat down to wait for the fish. His guest brought his fishing pole from the smaller boat, and was playing his fishing line in the water, knowing full well that there wasn't any bait on the end of the line, only a small weight.

"How ya been Harry?" His guest asked, but not really caring.

"Just fine. Yourself?" He said as he checked his own fishing line.

"Great."

"How's the land business?"

"A little slow this time of year, but it'll pick up after the first of the year."

"I s'pose." Then a tug on Harry's line signaled a bite. He stood and took his pole out of the gunwale mounted pole holder. And as he started to play the fish, his guest came up behind him and pushed him over board. Before Harry regained the surface of the cold water, the man onboard had stepped inside and gone forward to the boat's engine console. He took the boat off the autopilot and moved the throttle forward slightly increasing the boat's speed through the water.

On the nearby slow rolling surface of the water, Harry, without a life jacket on, shouted out, "For Christ's sake help me! I can hardly swim!"

"I remember," his guest said coldly as the boat had moved out of range. Harry couldn't reach it and he was too far from land to make any attempt to swim for it before he drowned.

"Please! Help me! Please!" The cold was already taking some effect on him.

"By bye, Harry." His guest said without emotion.

He waited until Harry slipped beneath the surface of the cold water. Then he motored the boat toward the west. When he was where he wanted to be, he took the engine out of gear and walked forward on the narrow side deck. His hands grabbed at any hand hold available as he went. Once on the foredeck he untied the anchor and its length of chain and line. He tied the end of the line off on a bow cleat and started to pay out the anchor line into the dark water. Once he had the boat anchored with the anchor line all the way out, it was slightly southeast of East point, about two hundred feet offshore in four fathoms of water.

He left the boat's engine running at an idle speed out of gear and the propane heater was still turned on. He did this so it would appear as if the details of anchoring the boat had not been finished.

A little later as a thick fog bank enveloped him and the boat, he lowered himself into the small fishing skiff he'd rented and cast loose from Harry's boat. He could hear the engine's slow rumble and the gurgle of the exhaust in the water as it lapped against the hull, as he moved silently away. He knew it would take him about an hour or so to get back from here.

The Queen's Knight takes his leave

R	N	B	Q	K	B	N	R
P	P	P	P	P	P	P	P
		$\mathcal{B}$		$\mathcal{P}$			
		$\mathcal{N}$	$\mathcal{P}$		$\mathcal{N}$		
$\mathcal{P}$	$\mathcal{P}$	$\mathcal{P}$			$\mathcal{P}$	$\mathcal{P}$	$\mathcal{P}$
$\mathcal{R}$		$\mathcal{B}$	$\mathcal{Q}$	$\mathcal{K}$			$\mathcal{R}$

N-QB3

FIRST MONDAY OF NOVEMBER
Frank had made the latest move on his chess board
while he ate his breakfast of hot oatmeal with brown
sugar on top of it like his mom had given him as a kid.
Looking at the board he didn't really know how anyone
else playing the black pieces would have responded,
he could only guess. The move he had read in the
morning paper was "N-QB3 ."

He had been experimenting with several different
moves for the black chess pieces over the past few
weeks but nothing seemed to fit, or could properly
combat the chess moves that the white chess player
had been making. Of course he was only guessing.
Now this new move, "Knight to Queen's Bishop three."

He thought as he looked at the chess game a few
minutes longer, then he got up from the table, lifted his
jacket off the back of the other chair and pulled it on.
He left his breakfast dishes filled full of water and a
drop or two of liquid soap in the pan full of water he
had used to cook his oatmeal in. The soap suds over
flowed the top of the pan. When Frank arrived at the
office, he took the elevator to the third floor and made
a bee line for Cary Ann's desk.

"Good Morning, Cary Ann," he said as he rounded her
desk.

"Morning, Frank." She looked up at him, liking his
appearance and sensing his rush.

"Morning reports in yet?"

"Sure, but I haven't printed them out yet so Sergeant
Brown doesn't have a copy either"

She turned to her left to face the computer, punched a key on the computer keyboard and brought up a menu on the computer screen. Then she pushed the down arrow key and scrolled down the column to the daily reports line and pushed the ENTER key. Within seconds the report came up on the screen. She then entered the command for three copies to be printed out and the printer along side the computer came to life.

As Frank waited for the reports, he noticed a picture of Cary Ann and a man standing on a dock by a boat. Curious, he said, "Nice picture."

"Yes, it's my father and our boat a few years ago."

Just as he was about to say something else, the printer finished printing out the morning reports. Cary Ann reached over and tore the reports off the printer. She pulled them apart at a seam and when she had them bundled into groups, she stapled them together and handed one to Frank.

"Here you go."

He leaned over her desk and quietly asked, "Would you like to have dinner at my place Thursday evening?"

She looked up into his pleading brown eyes. "I didn't know you could cook."

He grinned, "I'm not really a good cook, but I can make a great chef's salad."

"I think I'd like that." Then she added, "Can I bring something?"

"Just having you come will be treat enough," he said. She liked that thought as well.

Back at his desk Frank read through the few reports listed.

The first one was about a one car accident, which would not need him to look into. The second one would require his or Jim's attention. It was a domestic squabble, which resulted in a woman's death by gunshot. The husband was in custody. It was the third case that made him reach for his notebook. In it he wrote down the basics of the case.

Jacques Quine, Male Caucasian
This man's aircraft crashed into Puget
Sound His body, nor the aircraft have
been recovered. His aircraft was reportedly
kept in top condition so there is
questionable circumstances about
this accidental death.

Harry Ulman Male Caucasian,
Boat found at anchor southeast of East
point. This is a possible drowning. It
appears as if the owner, Harry Ulman
had attempted to anchor the boat but
fell overboard while doing so. An open
fishing tackle box was in the cockpit of the
vessel. The engine was running in idle as
the owner went forward to anchor the
vessel, falling overboard into the water.
The body has not been recovered.

Frank dismissed the first two cases, but the last two
held his attention. They were water related as had
been most of the recent accidental deaths in the area.
The missing aircraft he had known about, the other
one was unexpected.

"Jim, you need my help on anything today?"

"No, I don't. You?"

"No, not yet anyway, but my curiosity is beginning to get the best of me. It's about some accidental deaths that have been occurring. They seem to happen every other weekend, and when they do happen, and this is going to sound screwy, there's also been a chess move in the personal ad column of the newspaper as well.

"You still reading those?" Jim knew about Frank's interest in that part of the paper, but could never figure out why the interest.

"Yeah, and I've noticed these chess moves in a section of the paper where they wouldn't be easily found."

"Are you telling me you think they're related somehow?"

"I don't know. . . .I don't know, but it does seem odd that these chess moves coincide with a death each time."

"Okay, well I'm gonna go check on Joey again today, I'm hoping I can track him down. After that if you need a hand with anything, I'm available."

"Yeah, okay. Listen I've got a friend who used to be a chess whiz . . . I think I'll stop by and see him about the chess moves that have been appearing in the paper."

TED'S HOME

Frank parked as near the end of the long gravel driveway and as close to the house as he could. He would have parked nearer to the house but three of Ted's old cars blocked the driveway stopping him from going any farther. He had called Ted before leaving his apartment so that he would be expected.

As he started walking up the narrow and heavily overgrown pathway, he frequently had to duck his head down under an overhanging tree branch. The trees needed to be pruned, and all the grass around the home was in bad need of cutting. Frank wasn't sure if a regular lawn mower would cut it now, perhaps a chain saw might be more like the tool he needed. As he approached the house it appeared as if no one lived here, as if the house had been abandoned.

It had been many years since he had been to see Ted. They had talked by phone occasionally, but that was all. What he encountered when he arrived at Ted's home was the standing remnant of a home.

There had been a real home here, once, but now it was a strange sight. He knew that Ted was still living here. He also knew that Ted was one of those individuals that often started one project only to all of a sudden let the projects sit idle because of some new interest, but by most standards the condition of his home was ridiculous.

As he drew near the structure he could see that the exterior walls were only weather aged two-by-fours, their rich silver gray shapes struggling to hold up the roof. All the building's original siding had been removed from the house, also most of the interior wall material. He could barely see three or four rooms that still appeared intact in the central portion of the house.

Various kinds of rubble were still strewn around the area inside the perimeter of the house. A few pieces of plywood were leaning against one wall, some boxes of wiring near an open fuse panel as if the wiring portion was about to begin. A rusty table saw was around the corner of one of the remaining interior rooms.

It was as if Ted had just stopped for a quick cold beer and forgot to come back and start again. As he walked on what had once been a small concrete path, and as he neared the back of the house he called out, "Anybody home?"

After calling out twice, he heard Ted call to him from a distant out building. Ted came out of one of the buildings wiping his hands clean on an oily rag and greeted Frank with his hand extended. Then as he and Ted sat down in a couple of lawn chairs, he noticed that Ted didn't seem to have aged at all. Only his beard, now white and gray was the only indication he had aged at all. The laugh lines had been there all along. They spoke of times past when they had known one another on a much closer basis.

The main reason for Frank's visit today was because he had played a great deal of chess with Ted some years before when they were in school together. But Frank's ability in the game had not bloomed as Ted's had. Ted was one of those kind of chess players who devoted a great deal of time and study to the game. Frank just couldn't muster up enough curiosity about chess to play it as seriously.

After a few minutes of candid conversation, Ted said, "What can I do for you Frank?"

While they sipped a wine cooler fetched from somewhere in the remnants of the building behind him, Frank said, "Ted, I've come across something odd. I've been seeing chess moves in the paper where there have never been any chess moves. Also, each time one of these chess moves appears in the paper, someone dies an accidental death. At least they appear to be accidental."

"But you think there's more to it than that?"

"Well I'm not really sure, but I'd like your input." Frank then reached into his inside jacket pocket, pulled out a piece of paper and handed Ted the list of the chess moves to date.

Ted looked at the list briefly, then said, "Tell you what Frank, I'm involved in a project at the moment and don't have the time or mentality to really ponder the game right now. Why don't you let me think on 'em, and I'll give you a call when I've got something."

"Okay, but there is a time factor involved. There may be more deaths in the works."

EVERETT MARINA

Tom Schaeffer was in the small cabin area of the ferry when Frank arrived. His cup of hot coffee sat steaming on the control console nearby. As Frank knocked on the side of the ferry's hull, the knuckles of his right hand had felt the punishment from hitting them against the cold steel. Tom stuck his head out of the doorway and he looked down.

"Ahh, Mr. Chambers. I'm glad you could come by."

"Your message sounded important."

"Well, I don't know how important, but I remembered something that seemed odd about the conditions when Mr. Childes body was found here."

Frank was pleased that he might at last get a lead of some kind and said, "And what would that be?"

"The stern line wasn't cleated properly. It was loose, and the stern was too far away from the dock."

Frank was interested in boats, but not being a boater himself he didn't understand what was being said to him. "I don't understand."

"Here, I'll show you."

Tom walked down the ferry steps to get off the ferry deck to the dock, then he moved aft to the stern of the ferry and took the stern line loose from the docks mooring cleat. "Here's how I found the line."

He then looped the line around the cleat with several loops. "See. That's the way I found it."

"I see, but I still don't understand."

"Well, I never would leave a line like that. No boater would, because it wouldn't hold. After very much wave or tidal action, it would come loose."

"How would you leave it?"

Tom undid the line, then he showed Frank how a boater would put a locking loop over the cleat. "That's the proper method."

"You're saying someone else removed the line, then put it back on, but in the wrong manner?"

"That's exactly what I'm say'n."

FISHERMAN

The wind chill factor was well below zero, at least that's how it felt to David Long Horse. He didn't relish being out in the cold wind, but it was necessary. His drift net was all the way out and he was just in the process of recovering it. Fishing had not been good lately, so now he had to fish as often and as long as he could in the shortened fishing season just to make ends meet and that didn't always happen anymore.

He was nearing the end of a very long day. He had laid out his first net just before noon and it was now after ten o'clock that same night. The net was slowly rolling up onto the drum when suddenly he could hear the difference in the tension of the retrieving net as it wound up on the drum.

"Must have finally gotten a good catch," he said to no one. As the net came aboard, he watched over the stern of the boat down into the water, hopeful.

Then he saw it as it came into the beam of the stern lights as they played out over the water's surface. "What the. . . .h. . ." He reached over for the lever that stopped the hydraulic drive motor, then leaned over the stern. With his cold bare hands he pulled at the object.

"Oh, my God!" He let the bulky object slip back to the water's edge and went into the warmth of his deck house. He picked up the microphone from his VHF radio, keyed the mike and started what he knew would be a long process.

"Seattle Coast Guard, Seattle Coast Guard, Seattle Coast Guard, this is the fishing vessel Pegasus. Over."

Immediately the radio came alive, "This is Coast Guard group Seattle back to the vessel calling."

"Channel twenty two?"

"Seattle Coast Guard switched to channel twenty two."

He switched to the Coast Guard's working channel twenty-two and called them again. When they answered his call, he said, "Yeah, Seattle Coast Guard, I've been fishing off Lowell Point on Camano Island and I've just pulled a body up in my net."

The coast guardsman on watch said, "Stand by Pegasus." He then alerted the watch officer.

David waited for what seemed an eternity, when the Coast Guard finally came back. They said, "Pegasus, we have a Sheriff patrol boat from Everett and a Coast Guard cutter en route to your position. Can you standby?"

"Can do, Seattle Coast Guard. This is the fishing vessel Pegasus standing by channel twenty two."

David had had to slowly motor in place for a while. Then, disgusted, he'd gone forward and dropped his anchor to await the arrival of the Coast Guard and the Sheriff's department personnel. It was well over an hour before they arrived.

He'd been in constant touch with them by radio and when they'd arrived, he found himself and his vessel bathed in bright light from the deck of the Coast Guard cutter. The Sheriff's boat came along side his vessel and, with fenders out, they tied along his port side. His net, now hanging straight down, offered no resistance.

It took the Sheriff's deputies eighteen minutes of cumbersome wrestling to get the man's body onto a steel mesh stretcher affair that was lowered into the water. They apologized for having to cut his net to get the body free. He was glad it was them doing the work and not him. Sewing the net would be much easier than having to do what they had to do to get the body into the patrol boat from the water. Once they had the badly shredded body in the boat, it still wasn't easy getting it into a body bag. The stench was overwhelming.

The Blackburne Trap

R			Q	K	B	N	R
P	P	P			P	P	P
		N	P				
				P			
		B		P		B	
		N	P		N		
P	P	P			P	P	P
R		B	Q	K			R

Also known as the Black Death

HOME

Frank, being a true believer that to bring out the best flavor of a good chef's salad, you had to release the juices of all the ingredients by cutting them into small pieces. He diced the smoked ham slices, the sharp cheddar cheese, then sliced the celery into three long pieces using only the first two thirds of the stalk, then cut across them, making the long pieces into small chunks. The lettuce was cut into fairly small pieces as well. Bits of green pepper, some tomato, some tender parts of a couple of carrots, then he would offer her some Chinese rice vinegar to top it off. As he was putting the salad together, he was enjoying a glass of White Zinfandel wine. He usually drank white wine but Cary Ann had mentioned she drank White Zinfandel wines. It wasn't too bad, he thought.

Cary Ann arrived about six thirty and knocked softly on Frank's apartment door. Frank heard her from the kitchen, walked into the small entryway and opened the door, smiled and reached out his hand for her to come in. When she was inside, he took her coat and hung it in his small closet. When he turned back to her, she'd gone ahead into his living room. When he came up behind her, Cary Ann was looking at a picture of Miriam on a small table by the telephone. Frank had meant to put it away before Cary Ann arrived, but had forgotten.

"That's Miriam." He said, sensing her question. "We were married for seven years."

"I didn't know you had been married."

"Yes, well." He was at least able to talk about it now. For sometime after her death he hadn't been able to. "She was killed in a one car accident two years ago. She fell asleep at the wheel. . . . She suffered from Narcolepsy."

"Oh. I'm sorry, Frank."

"It's all right." Then he started walking past her. As he did so Cary Ann followed him into the kitchen. When she began to sit down at the table, she brushed lightly against him. Frank couldn't tell if it had been on purpose or not. Nervously he poured some wine for her into a chilled glass. He hadn't entertained a woman in his apartment since he had moved here after Miriam's death. He just hadn't found a woman that attracted him until now.

They were just finished with their chef's salad and on their third glass of wine, when he'd offered Cary Ann dessert. She turned it down saying she was just too full to enjoy it now. At the moment they were talking about her folks. "Yes, they still live in the house I was raised in."

"You never married." Frank had only heard this about her. Now he wanted to know, not that it would make any difference.

"No. It seems I was to busy pursuing a career." She was just in the process of telling him about how she had set herself certain goals she'd wanted to attain, when someone knocked on Frank's door.

"Who in the world could that be?" He got up from his chair and started toward the door saying, "Excuse me, be right back."

Cary Ann was feeling very comfortable with Frank. Better than she had felt with any man in sometime. He treated her like a woman and he was polite with her.

Frank reached out, turned the doorknob and pulled his apartment door open. She heard him say, "Oh, hi, Ted. Ahh . . . " Ted had noticed the hesitation in Franks voice. Frank didn't want to disturb the mood that had built between himself and Cary Ann, but Ted just didn't drop by, he was here for a reason. "Come in Ted. Come in"

When Ted got inside the door, he saw Cary Ann and sensed the interruption he was making. "I'm sorry to disturb you Frank, but I believe I have some chess game information you may want to know about."

It was too late. The mood had changed and they all knew it. "No, no, come on in." In the kitchen he pulled his chair out for Ted, introduced Ted and Cary Ann to one another, then went to his bedroom for another kitchen chair he kept in there out of the way.
Back in the kitchen, he sat on the chair he'd crowded between the other two chairs. This put him fairly close to the center of the table, the chair he was sitting on now blocked the narrow passage into, and out of the kitchen.

"Got a chess board, Frank?"

"Oh, sure." He'd forgotten to get it. He got up and turning slightly, reached behind him to retrieve the chessboard from the top of the refrigerator. It still had the pieces set up for the newspaper chess game.

With the board set up between the two of them Ted started his explanation of what he believed was happening in the chess game that was appearing in the morning paper. Ted set all the chess pieces back to their original starting positions, then he started from the beginning.

"Okay," he said. "The first move was white Pawn to King four correct?" Saying that, he consulted the notes on a piece of scratch paper he'd extracted from his coat pocket.

Frank had agreed, "That's right."

Then Ted said. "Okay what would be the normal opposing move?"

"Black would move Pawn to King four to block the white King's Pawn, keeping it from becoming a passed pawn," Frank said.

"Correct. Then white moved Knight to King's Bishop three to attack the black Pawn."

"Sure, then black would move Queen's Knight to Queen's Bishop three to counter the attack on his King's Pawn."

Frank looked at the board a few seconds trying to recall, then said, "It Looks like a standard Sicilian opening to me."

"To this point it is. Now, white moves the King's Bishop to Queen's Bishop four, attacking the black King's Bishop's Pawn."

"I would move the black Queen's Pawn to Queen three to protect the King's Pawn."

"And white moves Pawn to Queen three, as well."

"Then as black, I would move the Queen's Bishop to King's Knight five, pinning the White King's Knight."

"As would most other players," Ted said. " However, this is where it leaves the Sicilian opening and becomes the famed Blackburne opening." As his hand reached out and began the move he continued, "White moves Knight to Queen's Bishop three."

" Blackburne opening? I Never heard of it."

"Ahh, Frank if you had become a serious student of Chess you would know about this opening. It was a game played in Mid 1800s by Henry Blackburne. In reality it was developed by a man named, Legal, much earlier."

"So what happens?"

On Frank's list it looked like this.

White	Black
1 P-K4	P-K4
2 N-KB3	N-QB3
3 B-QB4	P-Q3
4 P-Q3	B-KN5
5 N-QB3	

"Make a move and I'll show you."

Frank moved Pawn to King's Rook three.

Ted reached out over the chessboard and moved the white King's Knight to King five, capturing the black King's Pawn.

Frank looked down onto the game in astonishment. Pleased with himself he said, "If you make that move, I can capture your Queen with the black Queen's Bishop."

"Correct, and without thinking, any greedy player would make the same move. However, if you make that move, as most players would, I'll move white King's Bishop to your King's Bishop two. With this move, by capturing your King's Bishop's Pawn, it'll place your King in check. Because of this move, you'll have no choice but to move the King to King two. Then I'll move my Queen's Knight to Queen five for check mate."

Frank looked on in amazement. Stunned he then said, "My God the Queen was just a sacrifice then."

"Exactly."

Frank realized that Cary Ann had been sitting quietly while the two of them had been mulling over this game of chess. "Oh, Cary I'm sorry. This is probably boring to you."

"Actually I'm finding it quite interesting. I play chess, so I'm following the game you're playing."

Frank smiled at her, his hand coming to a rest on top of hers, both of them feeling the warmth of this personal connection, and he said, "Thank you." He then turned back to Ted and asked, "Ted, what if I want'a make a counter move to this newspaper chess player. Any suggestions?"

"If you're going to do that, go with the one you just made and see what happens. We'll see what response you get, if any, and we'll go from there."

Ted looked at his watch. Realizing it was very late, he got up from the table without saying anything and went to Frank's closet to retrieve his coat.

Frank realized what Ted was doing, and got up to follow behind Ted saying, "Thanks for coming by Ted. I'll put the counter move in the paper tomorrow."

Ted stopped at the door, turned toward Cary Ann and said, "I'm not in any hurry to get home, so I can drop you somewhere if you like Cary Ann."

She smiled at him, then she said, "Thanks, but I'm staying for breakfast."

NEWSPAPER ADVERTISEMENT

Frank had asked the receptionist whom he should talk to concerning some advertisements that had appeared in the newspaper recently. He'd felt some resistance from her until he identified himself as a police officer. She had then made a quick phone call, and he was now sitting at a cluttered desk deep in the center of the newspaper's circulation department. The older woman sitting across from him at her desk, was in the process of searching through her computer data base for the information Frank had asked about.

"Yes, here it is." She read briefly through the information now displayed on the screen then continued. "It seems the advertisements you're asking about always came in the mail, with cash as payment. They have always been placed in the Saturday edition."

"Do you have an address on who sent them in?"

"Nothing."

"Isn't it required for you to know who's sending you advertisements?"

"No. Not if they fit in with the column requested, and if they're not pornographic."

After he thought about it for a few moments, "Okay. Here's what I'd like you to do for me. First if, or when, you get another one of these chess move advertisements, contact me at my office as soon as you can." He handed her one of his police business cards.

"Second, I want you to place this advertisement in the personals section of the paper for this Friday and Saturday. He handed her a slip of paper that had the chess moves on it, 5. N-QB3 -- P-KR3.

"Do you want me to refuse to print the other chess move if I get one?"

"Absolutely not. If they come in print them. Just notify me when you get them, and save the envelope and its contents for me as well."

"Very well, Mr. Chambers."

The Competition

R			Q	K	B	N	R
P	P	P			P	P	
		N	P				P
				P			
		B		*P*		B	
		N	*P*		*N*		
P	*P*	*P*			*P*	*P*	*P*
R		*B*	*Q*	*K*			*R*

P-KR3

COMPETITION

He was thinking, *'What the hell is going on?'* He just happened to look at the personal ad section and saw the chess move he had inserted in the paper the week before. Now, however, a counter move appeared. His move wasn't supposed to run two weeks in a row, and he had never even considered that someone would answer it with an opposing move.

He was upset over this situation. "I wonder if this is some kind of joke."

He began to search his mind, trying to place the opposing counter move on the chessboard in his mind. Then he thought, *'It would have to be a serious player. The move was the correct one to have been played.'* He couldn't be sure if it was just someone playing a joke, or if it was some serious chess buff.

His curiosity was taking a mental toll on him, and now he was pacing slowly around his den. He'd only put the chess moves in the paper for his own satisfaction. Just a mental part of him that wanted to say publicly, "I know how this damn game comes out. But you don't."

Stopping now as he paced, he would look down at the chessboard he'd set up, the ornate chess pieces of gold and silver glimmering in the light. The heavy polished stone chessboard was firmly anchored in place on the table. He had placed the move from the newspaper on the board and confirmed it again. His head tilted slightly as he looked. *'Not a bad chess move.'* Also, it was not a threatening move, at least not yet.

Again he began pacing slowly around the room. There was no way he could tell if something was going on until after he made his next move. He felt some excitement growing within him. Was it fear, or a challenge? That part wasn't clear to him yet. The decision had already been made to send his next move in the mail so it would appear in the Saturday paper.

BANK

In his mind he was sorting through it all again. He sifted through every step repeatedly. Still, he couldn't find a fault anywhere in his actions. Everything had gone according to plan. He was aware of Marty's habit of going out to the place on the island and had waited for him that morning. He'd made a point of greeting Marty casually when Marty had come out of the ferry cabin when he'd called out to him. He'd asked Marty for a hand up and when Marty had offered his hand, he had just pulled him slightly. It just happened that Marty had fallen easier than he had expected. When Marty fell, he'd hit his head on the mooring bit the ferry was tied to. Although it had saved him the trouble of killing him, he had only to untie the line, push Marty into the water and walk away.

Then when he'd gone to see Harold, he'd parked down the road from Harold's house. He hadn't seen another car or person, coming or going, on his drive into the small private area.

Clyde had been really easy and there hadn't been anyone else around. Clyde had seemed very receptive to meeting him on the bridge. He knew Clyde liked shooting photos of everything around him and he figured Clyde would take the opportunity to get some good photos from the bridge.

A voice interrupted his thoughts. "Next." Finally it was his turn at the counter. He stepped up to the banking window where the young lady waited. "Good morning, Sir," she said.

"Good morning. I'd like this in cash." He passed her a personal check. She looked at it, smiled, and asked for his identification. He gave her his bank card and his drivers license.

"Just a moment please," she said. Then she took the check to the head cashier who looked at the check, then at the customer. "Oh, yes, it's all right. He called me earlier and it's been approved. I'll bring you the necessary funds in just a moment."

The young woman returned to her position, handed him his drivers license and his bank card, saying, "it'll be just a moment, Sir."

A few moments later the head cashier came to the cashier's position where he waited. He watched as she slowly counted out the cash in one hundred dollar bills. "There you are. Two hundred and seventy five thousand dollars."

"Thank you." He paused long enough to stuff the bundles of cash into a cloth bank bag.

"You're aware that that almost closes your account?" the head teller added.

"Yes, but the man I'm dealing with today will only accept cash for his piece of land. Kind'a eccentric, but that's what he wants."

EVANS

The Mukilteo ferry had just pulled into its slip and docked a few minutes before. The crew had finished unloading the walk on passengers and the bicyclists. Now as they were letting the automobiles start to unload two rows at a time, there seemed to be a problem near the rear of the ferry. The deck supervisor went aft to see what was going on. He found one car near the end of the ferry without a driver in it. Concerned, he got on a nearby inter-ship telephone and called the bridge.

The captain answered the line on the second ring saying, "Bridge here."

"Skipper, this is Jimmy. We've got a car down here on the center deck without any driver. What'ya want'a do about it?"

"Damn . . . Well route traffic around it, while I make an announcement over the speaker system. You stay put nearby, okay?"

Over the speaker system Jimmy heard, "ALL PASSENGERS WITH AUTOMOBILES MUST RETURN TO THEIR VEHICLES IMMEDIATELY."

All the other cars had gone, yet this one car was still on board without a driver. The deck crew received their instructions from the Captain on the bridge. They were to keep anyone from boarding the ferry until the situation with the abandoned car was resolved.

On the dock, the ferry parking lot was full of traffic waiting patiently to come aboard, not knowing that their trip was going to be put on hold for sometime.

The crew knew the daily ferry schedule was slowly going down the tube.

Jimmy was speaking over the inter-ship telephone with the Captain on the bridge about the conditions at the moment. "We found a jacket on the port side of the after deck. It had some receipts in one pocket made out to a Mr. Richard Evans. But we haven't found him, or anyone else, connected with that automobile yet."

"Well, keep looking for him. The Coast Guard has started a search of the area and they have enlisted several pleasure craft in the area as well."

"Very well, Sir," he said and returned to making his rounds of the crew who were searching every nook and cranny on the ferry boat. Three hours and seventeen minutes later the search was canceled. One small boat in the area had turned up a brown hat found afloat in the area that the ferry would have passed through. A bubble of air trapped beneath the brim was all that kept it afloat. The local police patrol had the car towed to the police compound for later holding and the Coast Guard had concluded that if someone had fallen over board, he could not have survived the frigid waters of the sound any longer than this. It was only speculation that perhaps someone had picked him up in one of the many boats that ply these waters.

The Error, or Sacrifice?

R			Q	K	B	N	R
P	P	P			P	P	
		N	P				P
				N			
		B		*P*		B	
		N	*P*				
P	*P*	*P*			*P*	*P*	*P*
R		*B*	*Q*	*K*			*R*

N-K5XP

THIRD MONDAY IN NOVEMBER

Frank woke before his alarm went off. He turned over, and was trying to get comfortable, but couldn't. "Damn." He hated it when he woke up having to go the bathroom before the alarm went off. He could have slept longer but he was awake and knew he probably couldn't go back to sleep now. Once he woke up, his mind had shifted into gear, and his mind these days was being occupied with what he thought was a new serial or revenge killer.

He unlocked his apartment door, still naked because he hadn't taken time to get a bathrobe before making the trip to the bathroom. He opened the door slightly, and peeked out into the hallway to see if anyone was around. Once he was sure there wasn't anyone, he opened the door quickly reached out and down to pick up his morning paper. The cool air from the hallway quickly chilled him. Once back inside he went to the kitchen and started the coffee and left the paper on the kitchen table.

He shaved first so the shower wouldn't fog up the mirror, then he took a hot shower, mostly just to warm up and then he got dressed. Back in the kitchen he poured a bowl full of cold cereal, some milk but no sugar and began eating it while he read the paper. Only now he had changed his reading habits and turned to the personal ads first.

There he saw it, the ad he dreaded. It read, 5 - P-KR3, followed by 6 N-K5XP. Frank was sure someone had died in the last day or so.

119

OFFICE

Not surprised, Frank found his parking place had someone else's car in it, so he parked in Jim's spot. As he had arrived earlier than usual, he was sure that whoever parked in his place would be gone by the time Jim came to work, at least he hoped so. The other two spots allotted to the detective squad usually had the cars that Kim Larson, and Don Olson used on their night shift.

On his desk he found a message from the woman at the newspaper office about the chess move in the newspaper for the weekend. It was too late for her to tell him now, he'd already read it in the newspaper, but he knew she had wanted to warn him ahead of time. Frank dug into his desk drawer and pulled out the list of names of the recent deaths he had become concerned with. Without thinking or really looking at the names, he had listed them on a sheet of paper in the order that their deaths had occurred.

Later when Cary Ann arrived, Frank was waiting for her in the coffee shop. Frank was here in the guise of business but he really wanted to be near her. He wanted to touch her and enjoy the feelings that passed through their touch when it happened. She saw him when she came in. Smiling, she poured herself a cup of coffee, then joined him eagerly.

"We still on for dinner next Friday night?" she asked.

"You bet we are." Their relationship, now well established, left Frank feeling he didn't have to hesitate in any conversation with her any longer.

Then he added, "Cary, later in the morning would you do me a favor and run some names through your system for me. When you can, that is?"

"Is this pertaining to what is becoming known around the office as your chess killer case?"

He had been aware that there was some talk about his fascination with what were to others, seemingly accidental deaths. "Yes. I'm pretty sure that several of these accidental deaths are connected somehow and I'm having problems finding the link."

Some time after they finished their coffee together and Frank was again back in his office, Cary Ann opened the door, peeked her head in saying, "You may want to look at this report before you give me your list of names."

She handed him the morning computer printout. Part of it read:

Richard Evans Male - Caucasian
May have fallen overboard off the Mukilteo
ferry. Personal automobile found on
board. His Jacket with his identification
was found by the railing.

A boater found a hat, possibly belonging
to Mr. Evans floating in the sound. The
Coast Guard Search failed to find a body.

Frank picked up the list of names he was attributing to the chess killer, and penciled in the name Richard Evans at the bottom of the list. Then he gave the list to Cary Ann.

"This is the list I'm curious about. If your computer system can supply me anything useful, I'd like any info you can get me."

Harold Childes
Harry Hanson
Clyde Elders
Jacques Quine
Harry Ulman
Richard Evans

"I can't do it until I've finished my routine items for the day."

"No problem, and thanks, Cary." After Cary Ann had left, Frank added the latest information into his notebook.

Back at her desk Cary Ann started to type the names into her computer terminal. She typed them in last name first, and first name last, as that would be how the search would look for them. After she finished typing the last name on the list, something struck her as odd, though it didn't register right away. When she'd finished putting in the data, and while she waited for the results to come back and be printed out, she smiled. "Aha," she said out loud startling Joline at the desk next to hers. She saw what it was that had captured her interest. The first letters of each name on the list, spelled a word.

OFFICE

Jim had been trying to tell Frank he had finally tracked Joey down. He finally broke through Frank's train of thought.

"Oh, I'm sorry, I was somewhere else. So where'd you find him?"

"He's been in the lock up in Marysville."

"What was he picked up for?"

"For suspicion of burglary."

"If he's guilty, his future is pretty well figured out isn't it?"

"Yep. Back in the slammer."

"Jim." Frank wanted to interrupt Jim to have him consider some ideas. "I've been following some odd circumstances lately that I'd like to run by you."

"You mean the accidental deaths you've been curious about?"

"Yes, but right now, I'm not sure they're necessarily accidental deaths."

At this point in their conversation Cary Ann walked into their office and handed Frank his list of names, also the computer list of information she had found on each name. The top cover sheet had the name's Frank had given her. The next sheet down, her list of names, were last names first, the reverse of what Frank had given her.

She said to him, "Odd thing about this list of names you gave me. That is, it's odd about the order of the names, not necessarily the information about them."

"What'dya mean?"

"Take a look."

Frank looked at the list and said, "So?"

"Don't you think that it's odd that the initials of their last names spells a word?"

Frank looked at the list again.

Childes, Marty
Hanson, Harry
Elders, Clyde
Quine, Jacque
Ulman, Harry
Evans, Richard

Frank took a piece of nearby scratch paper and wrote the initials down in the order she had indicated, then looked at it. C-H-E-Q-U-E, "My God. Isn't that strange? It spells CHEQUE."

His mind sorting through the letters. He remembered the book on chess in the attache case belonging to Marty childes, and the fact that Jacque Quine was deeply involved in the game as well. Then he thought, *'Could this be used the same way to spell CHECK as in CHECK mate?'* His mind was racing now. If this was the case, he knew there could be at least four more murders disguised as accidents.

LAW OFFICE

Frank had gone to Ted's law office after Ted's secretary had called asking if he could stop by. It seemed strange being here in Ted's office. Compared to his home, Ted's office was like a clean room at some space lab. Maybe it was just his secretary's doing that kept the place so clean and uncluttered.

While he was there, they had gone over the chess game several times trying different moves in answer to what had been made previously in the newspaper. They were both very aware of the devastation that would take place if the black Bishop captured the white Queen. If that move was made, the game would be over in two more moves. Frank was stalling for time. He didn't know whether to make that move and let the game come to an end, or try to avoid it. Ted was murmuring something.

"I'm sorry, Ted. What were you saying?"

"I'm suggesting that you capture the white Knight on his King five square."

"Humm," Frank muttered as he studied the chess board. "The Queen's Pawn could move from Queen three and capture it."

"Yes, but if you use the Pawn to capture the Knight, the white Queen can then capture your black Bishop."

Frank studied the board a few more moments, then said, "You're right. How about we capture the white Knight with our black Knight on Queen Bishop three."

"That's a much better move, because then it'll protect the black Bishop on your King's Knight five. This'll put pressure on your opponent because then his Queen will still be under attack."

The Unexpected!

R			Q	K	B	N	R
P	P	P			P	P	
			P				P
				N			
		$\mathcal{B}$		$\mathcal{P}$		B	
		$\mathcal{N}$	$\mathcal{P}$				
$\mathcal{P}$	$\mathcal{P}$	$\mathcal{P}$			$\mathcal{P}$	$\mathcal{P}$	$\mathcal{P}$
$\mathcal{R}$		$\mathcal{B}$	$\mathcal{Q}$	$\mathcal{K}$			$\mathcal{R}$

N-K4XN

COMPETITION

His feelings were mixed as he read the morning paper. There it was. A counter move had been made to the one he placed in the paper the weekend before.

6 N-K5XP ------ N-K4XN

He'd gone to his chessboard, made the move he found in the paper, and still he was disappointed. Discouraged by the fact that his opponent hadn't captured his Queen, which is what the unsuspecting and greedy player would have done. At the same time he was excited about the potential of the game at hand, even though it upset his original game plan. He rose from the chair, walked away, then returned to review the move from the newspaper on his chess board again. He looked at it for several minutes, started to move one of his chess pieces, but didn't.

Suddenly he decided to leave the decision as to what he should do about this unexpected move for later. He still had to complete the new plans he was outlining in his mind for Rick. He felt he had a good idea for this one as well. So far no one had seemed the wiser as to what he had done. In his mind he knew that it wouldn't be much longer until he could move ahead and start life anew.

OFFICE

Frank had received the envelopes and the contents from the newspaper office early in the day. He had then taken them personally to the Seattle document examination office for a work up. The results were not promising, and he knew it before hand. There were several finger prints on both the envelopes, which was to be expected, but only one set on the inside page which were confirmed to be those of the woman at the newspaper office who had accepted the ad in the first place.

The document's examination office's real job was to find the source of the paper on which the advertisement, as it had been received, was printed on, and any other information they could glean from it. It turned out it was standard computer print out paper that could be obtained in any one of several hundred computer supply stores. The print on the paper was believed to be from a dot matrix printer, most likely a nine pin printing head. The type of printer was unknown but they were sure it was one of a type no longer in production.

"A blank. Just a damn blank wall," he said to no one. He was just disgusted with the lack of any hard evidence on what he thought was a definite case of several murders.

Frank then read the information again that Cary Ann had supplied him about the six deaths he was almost sure now must be connected. As yet he had no proof of this, but because of the corresponding chess moves in the newspaper he was pretty certain this was the case.

After he finished reading the files again, he set them aside. So far he could not positively link the six men together physically. He was pretty sure that they had not known each other on a personal basis, at least not with a continuing social life together.

He had Jim helping him with some of the research work now and, after many phone calls, Jim had found out from friends or relatives that all six of the accident victims were strong chess players. Now Jim was going to check into the financial back ground of each man to find out if there was any connection between them in the business community.

At a loss as to where to look next, Frank decided to get out of the office for a while. Before he was out of the building, he stopped to talk with Sergeant Brown. Finished with the brief conversation, he was just about to leave the office, when Jim called out to him from their office. "Frank. There's a long distance phone call for you."

He walked briskly and, as Frank entered the office, he asked Jim," Got any idea who it is?"

"Mrs.Bradshaw, from Nanaimo, Canada."

Picking up the receiver, he said, "Mrs. Bradshaw. Frank Chambers here."

"Yes, Mr. Chambers. Last night just before going to sleep I happened to think of something about the big chess game my father played in."

Frank's heart rate picked up a little in anticipation and he interrupted her, "Someone's name perhaps?"

"No, but I did remember that the yacht they played the chess tournament on, was a charter yacht. I believe it was from some charter company north of Seattle."

"Do you know the name of the boat by chance?"

"No. I'm not sure I ever knew it. Sorry that's about all I recall at the time."

"Would you have any idea who chartered the boat?"

"I'm sorry. I don't have the foggiest idea."

One final thought ran through his mind, "Do you recall when the game was played?"

"Umm, yes. I think it took place about the second week of July. I remember, because it was after Canada Day."

Frank thanked her and hung up the phone. He turned to Jim asking, "What the blazes is Canada Day?"
Jim grinned saying, "It's like our fourth of July."

"Oh . . . Well, we may have just gotten a direction to start following up."

FIRST MONDAY IN DECEMBER

Jim arrived at the office just after nine thirty in the morning. Frank was in the process of making phone calls to one of the many marine charter companies in the Puget Sound area. Apparently, from the conversation that Jim over heard, Frank wasn't having any luck. As Jim hung his jacket up on the coat rack behind the door, Frank hung up the phone and looked at Jim, grinning.

Jim could see Frank was excited about something, so he asked, "What?"

"No one died this last weekend."

"No one?" He knew that had to be wrong.

"Well, no one that's connected with this group of deaths I've been following."

"So, why would there be anyone die who's connected to that group of people?"

"One reason is that its been two weeks since the last one died that was, or is, connected to this case, which tells me someone was due to die in the last couple of days or so. At least that's how the trend had been going. But the main reason I say this is because there was another chess move in the paper this morning."

"You're sure it's the same person playing?"

"Oh, sure.The woman from the newspaper confirmed it was the same style of computer printout and the same style of ad she'd received in the past moves."

"So what does it all mean?" Jim wasn't quite following Frank's line of thinking.

"I dunno yet, but it could mean that we've given the community two more weeks of time against the death chess player."

THE THIRD MONDAY OF DECEMBER

Frank had hardly slept a wink during the night. He couldn't sleep because his head itched, his body itched and he knew he needed to take a shower to put a stop to it. This was a condition he encountered whenever he slept too warmly. Frank had been in touch with the newspaper before he had gone to bed the night before and there was no news.

Then, in the early morning hours, and even though he hadn't been listening for him, he heard the paper boy leave the paper at his apartment door. As he wasn't sleeping anyway, Frank decided to get up. When he got to the door of his apartment and opened it, he could still hear the paperboy's footsteps fading away as he reached down for his paper.

Frank's bare feet padded the floor softly as he went into the kitchen to put the coffee on to percolate. While the coffee started, he went to get showered, shaved and dressed. He finished his shower, but the coffee was ready before he was. In the kitchen he removed the pot from the stove and poured his first cup.

As he sat at his kitchen table, the light brown cushion on the chair slid off onto the floor. He reached down for it, thinking, *'Maybe I can get Cary to sew some tie strings onto these things for me.'*

With his fingers fumbling he opened the paper to the personal ads. When he finished reading them, he said out loud, "HOT DAMN, NO MOVE!"

Smiling now he rose from the table he went to the refrigerator to get some eggs and sausage links. It took only a few minutes before he had a hot breakfast in front of him.

'Now,' he thought, *'I can enjoy something to eat.'* After he finished his meal, he washed his dishes in lukewarm water as it took too long for the hot water to get to his apartment, and he was impatient to get to the office. He had a busy day planned.

GAME

Just as they were finishing lunch, Cary Ann placed her hand on top of Frank's. "Thanks for lunch, Frank."

Her feelings were growing deeper for him as they spent more time together. They both felt the excitement of being together as if drugged and needing more.

"My pleasure." They could both feel the warmth of love flowing from one another through their hands. "I suppose we better get back, huh?"

On their way back to the office Frank stopped in front of one of the small shops they were passing, then he led her by the hand into the shop. He looked around the shelves briefly until he found what he was looking for and purchased a small inexpensive chess set that contained a cardboard chess board inside covered with red and black squares. The kind of board that doubles as a checker board as well. Cheap hollow plastic chess pieces inhabited a divided container on one side of the box, checkers on the other side.

Once he was back in his office he set the chess game up on a small table he'd gotten from the office supply room. He laid a slip of paper on the small table next to the chess board, then played the game up to the present move that had been the last one made in the newspaper, all the respective pieces in their proper locations.

He'd purchased this chess set principally for his own benefit. He felt as though his mind might be more in tune with the situation if he had to face it, so to speak, on a daily basis. As if it might somehow, as if by magic, tell him what he needed to know about the other player.

Over a period of a few days most of the other chess players in the office got wind of it and would stop by to see what the latest move had been. Often they would come into his office and stand in silence just mulling the game over in their own minds. Sometimes, if Frank was out of the office, they would leave him notes as to their thoughts about the game and what they considered the next best move.

Sometimes they would leave questions as to why he had made this move or that one. Most had fallen into the trap of taking the white Queen with the black Bishop as he had considered in the beginning. None of them, however, had any idea of how to find the killer he was after. Frank had begun to think that having the game set up in his office was almost more of a deterrent, than a help because of the ongoing interruptions.

One day after he came back from a morning out of the office investigating an ATM hold up that had been solved quickly and easily. The thief had held the woman up at the teller machine, and he had just made a twenty dollar withdrawal from his own account. They had him on tape for both occasions, then with his credit card information they had tracked him down and arrested him. As Frank approached his office he heard voices as he drew near.

"I'm telling, you he should have moved the Queen's Rook Pawn out one square to stop any attack on that side."

"Not a chance. If he did that, he would lose the advantage. The result would put him down a move."

"You guys are both wrong. He should have moved . . "

As Frank entered the room, they looked up, one of them saying, "Well Frank we've almost got your game solved." They all chuckled over that comment, but he knew they didn't have a clue.

As the days passed he became aware of other chess sets appearing in several locations throughout the office. Some adorning corners of desks, one on top of a file cabinet and one on top of a bookcase. All were following his game.

SEARCHING

Frank and Jim had agreed on the areas each of them
would call. Once again they were trying to come up
with some information about the large motor yacht that
had been used for the chess game. At least now they
knew one had been chartered for the million dollar
chess game in Nanaimo, British Columbia the year
before. Frank was calling the charter companies on
the south and west side of Puget Sound, while Jim
was calling the ones on the north and east sides.

Frank had drawn blanks on his first three phone calls.
His luck was failing at finding anyone who had big
motor yachts for charter. The one he had just finished
talking to did charter large sailboats, but no power
boats of any size to speak of. Jim was having about
the same kind of luck with his telephone calls. Just
before the two men were ready to quit for lunch, Jim's
last call was giving him the feeling that perhaps he
was onto a possible lead. The charter company he had
been talking with didn't charter large motor yachts but
had suggested that he call the ULTIMATE YACHT
CHARTER CO. in Anacortes, Washington.

He called information for the number, then when he
finished dialing it, a young sounding man answered
the phone, "ULTIMATE YACHTS." The man sounded
quiet and unconcerned.

"Yes, this is Jim Parsons with the Sheriff's Office. I'd
like to speak to the manager please."

Jim could almost see the guy straighten up in his
chair, his voice now more concerned. "I'm sorry sir, but
the manager won't be back from lunch until one
o'clock or so."

Not wanting to wait until the manager came back, Jim asked, "Can you tell me if you folks charter large power boats?" Jim looked at his watch again, he and Frank would be late for lunch.

"Yessir, some very large boats."

"Would you know if you chartered one last year in July?"

"Yessir, we charter them out all year long."

"Would you know if one of them went to Canada last July?"

"I haven't any idea. I'm new here. You'd have to ask Mr. Jenkins about that."

Jim was getting the idea that he wasn't going to make much more head way with this guy. So he asked "How many large power boat charter companies like yourselves are there in the area that you're aware of?"

The young man said with pride, "None that have boats as big as ours."

"Thanks." Then as an after thought he added, "Would you tell Mr.Jenkins to stay at the office this afternoon. We'll be up to talk with him."

"Yessir, I'll tell him when he gets back."

After he hung up, Jim said to Frank, "Well, Buddy, I think we've got a hot one. Let's take a ride."

CHARTER OFFICE

It was mid afternoon when the two of them entered the yacht charter office, and they spotted Mr.Jenkins right away. He was the only one who seemed to be nervous, as if he knew they were police officers. He stood up from behind his desk and approached them. "You the fella's from the Sheriff's Office?"

"That's right. I'm Frank Chambers, and this is Jim Parsons." Frank offered his identification but Mr. Jenkins didn't bother to even glance at it, apparently quite satisfied by Frank's word.

He then turned slightly and motioned to his right, "This way, gentlemen."

Frank and Jim followed his lead into a small, but very comfortable conference room. There was an oval oak table in the center of the room with plush chairs surrounding its perimeter. "Coffee?" he asked.

"Please." Frank said.

"No, thanks." Jim followed.

"Mr. Jenkins we . . . " He was interrupted.

"Please, call me Carl."

"Fine . . . Carl, we're looking for some information about a large motor yacht that you may have chartered out last year, about July I think."

"Which one?"

"I don't know," Frank continued.

"You keep records of all your charters don't you, Carl?" Jim asked.

"Oh, sure. It would just be easier if I knew which boat it was you wanted to know about."

Frank continued, "It would be a large yacht and would have gone to Nanaimo, British Columbia for a period of time in July."

"Ahhh." He sounded like this brought back a memory. "Just a minute." He got up from his chair and left the office. When he returned, he had several file folders in his hands.

"These are the only boats we had that were officially allowed into Canada last year."

As they reviewed the files together, the third one caught their attention. The "Largo," a hundred and thirty five feet in length, had been chartered the third week of June and had not been returned to the charter company until the third week of July. After Frank and Jim read the file, both agreed this was most likely the boat they were after. Carl went to the conference room door and called out, "Robbert would you go get the log book from the Largo for me?"

A young man got up from a corner desk and hurriedly left the office. He returned a few minutes later out of breath, came into the room and handed the leather bound volume to Carl.

"Thank you," Carl said "If I need anything else I'll call you."

"Yessir." The young man turned and left the room, closing the door quietly behind him as he left.
Jim recognized the voice as the one he had spoken to on the phone earlier in the day.

Reading through the log book Carl said, "She cleared Canadian customs at Bedwell Harbour, Canada early June 26th, then spent two days at anchor in Montague. On the 29th of June she was moored at the outer public dock at Nanaimo, Canada. She apparently stayed at this location until the 15th of July. Ummm . . . Then she returned to Roche Harbor at San Juan Island to clear customs back into the states and then returned here to our docks.

"Who chartered the boat?" Frank asked, his note book open.

Carl leafed through the file folder, finally pulling out a charter agreement. "Mr. Andrew Tatum of Friday Harbor, Washington."

"How did he pay for the charter?" Jim asked.

Carl scanned down the file again and said. " A platinum charge card was used. However, when Mr. Tatum's charter account was paid in full, his check of fifty thousand dollars was returned to him."

"Why would he have a check for fifty thousand dollars returned to him?"

"Deposit."

"Oh, of course." Frank mentioned more in fun than anything. He couldn't imagine having fifty grand to use as a deposit on anything. "Is that a standard deposit?"

"Oh no. Sometimes it's much more but Mr. Tatum is a repeat customer. He charters a large yacht from us every five years. We never question his account, or his method of payment to us."

TATUM INTERVIEW

Frank arrived at the Tatum home just after ten in the morning. The large home sat back from the main paved road some distance. The driveway appeared to have originally been asphalt. It also didn't seem to have had any real care since being put in place originally. The small rocks, which originally had been encased in asphalt, were now mostly loose gravel with weeds beginning to take hold at various locations along its circular length.

Frank parked behind the large Black Lincoln that was inside one cubical in a large three car garage. The garage housed the Lincoln, a small fishing boat on a trailer and cardboard cartons plus a few wooden boxes stacked to the ceiling in the third space. The garage doors were open to the elements of mother nature.

Frank walked up the brick walkway, the cold of the morning biting at his ears. The bricks had been set up on a sand and mortar base. Then they were spaced apart slightly, the gaps filled with the same sand and mortar mix, and wet down with water until it set up into a solid unit. Frank pushed the doorbell and he could hear it chime inside the home. An elderly Spanish woman stood at the door when it opened. When she answered the door, she was drying her hands on an apron tied loosely around her waist.

As Frank showed her his identification her eyes widened with concern, then he said, "Mr. Tatum porfavor." He could see some relief on her face, and he understood her natural fear of law enforcement officials. He knew most immigrants were afraid of the police because of the treatment they received in their own home countries.

145

"Si." She moved to one side indicating he should come in.

She led the way to a large den, or a small library, Frank couldn't be sure which. Ushering him inside, she said, "Uno momento." Then she left him alone.

While he waited, Frank admired eight ornate chess sets housed in a well lit glass cabinet against one wall. The wall paneling was done in a rich rose wood. The book shelves nearby were crammed full of chess books of every kind. Some of them had apparently been purchased years ago, some of them new, indicating a continual updating of the current works. The plush dark green carpeting and dark green upholstery covered chairs added immensely to the rich interior. A large teak wood desk occupied an area overlooking the sound. A ferry was working its way into the harbor heading for the ferry dock.

About ten minutes later a man about fifty, or fifty five, entered the room, his dark hair still damp from a very recent shower. He eyed Frank curiously and introduced himself.

"I'm Andy Tatum. My house keeper says you wanted to see me?"

"Yessir. I'm sorry to bother you this early in the day, unannounced, but I need some information from you about a boat you chartered last June from Ultimate Yacht Charters."

"Yes. That would be the Largo. We had her for about a month."

"We?"

"Yes there's a group of us that charter a large boat for a social get together every five years."

"That's to play chess, is it not?" Frank watched Mr. Tatum's expression as he said this. It was one of surprise, but not one of alarm.

"Well. . . . yes, that's correct. But there is a great deal of other social activity that takes place as well."

"I'm sure there is, but your primary reason for this gathering was to play chess was it not?"

"Basically, that's correct."

Andrew Tatum indicated two nearby chairs, and after they had sat down, Frank explained to Tatum the reason he had come to see him. "So as you can see Mr. Tatum, I believe these are homicide cases, not accidental deaths as we are supposed to believe."

His replies to Frank's questions were showing concern and some excitement as Andrew had begun to see the pattern. As Frank continued asking questions of Andrew Tatum he wasn't getting as much information as he would like. Andrew wasn't withholding information, just giving Frank some personal information, but most of it Frank already knew about.

"How did this group of people get along with each other?"

147

"You mean the group of chess players themselves?"

"Yes."

"I believe they had a good time. We drank a lot, had guests aboard and played chess, of course."

"Any problem with any of the guests?"

"None."

"How many guests did you have aboard?"

"Oh, that would vary from day to day."

"Am I to understand then, that the group got along okay and that there weren't any problems with any guests either?"

"That's correct."

"Did the group of people you had aboard entertain a lot?"

"No, goodness no. They didn't have time to entertain. I mean they played chess most days. You know, for the elimination of the weaker players."

"As you would in any normal chess match?"

"Yes, of course. . . . They would average about five games a day building up to the final chess match for the championship and the prize money."

"I understand the purse is usually quite large?"

"Always the same amount."

"One million dollars, I understand?"

"That's correct. However, the game is not known publicly."

"Who won the game?"

"Mr. Eldridge. . . . Harvey Eldridge."

Frank wrote the winners name in his notebook. "Who'd he play against?"

"Richard Evans was his last opponent."

Frank leaning back in his chair, thought for a moment, knowing Richard Evans was on his list of accident victims but Eldridge wasn't. Then he asked, "How is it you are the individual who charters the boat for each chess match?"

"Actually I started doing it for the group some years ago. It went so well the first time we did it that it just seemed to become my responsibility each time after that."

Frank continued, "I'm lead to believe that the referee was the only other person to receive any sort of cash payment for his efforts in this chess match as well?"

"That's correct. Last year, as referee, I received about seventy thousand dollars after paying all the expenses and the charter fees."

This surprised Frank. He hadn't expected this turn of events. "I didn't know you were the one who refereed the games."

"Oh, yes. I have been the referee for every million dollar chess game tournament as a matter of fact."

"How is it, as a referee, you received such a high salary?"

"It's never a fixed fee, I'm expected to keep whatever is left after the main prize of one million dollars is paid out and after the bills are paid. I'm more than just a referee. I arrange everything for the charter and take care of all debts we incur. The charter company, the professional crew, the caterer, sometimes the entertainment, everything."

"And you referee the games as well."

"Yes, I do. Occasionally I might play a few chess games to help one player or another to get warmed up for a match, but basically I am there to referee the chess matches."

"Were there any problems in any of the chess matches on this trip?"

"Oh no, my decision on a game is always final. The games being played are either won or lost. Once in a while we would have a draw, but anything requiring my decision was always final and without any question."

"Kind of a position of power, isn't it?"

"Not really. Well, perhaps. More one of mutual respect. You see I never play favorites, and they all know that."

Before Frank left Mr. Tatum's home he asked for, and received, a list of the players that had participated in the chess match. Of the players who had played in the final tournament, there were only three left alive.

As he was about to go out the door he turned back and said, " Mr. Tatum, I'd be careful and be aware of who's around you, if you get my meaning."

EVENING

Cary Ann had arrived just after six o'clock, tired from her long day at work. She and Frank were just finishing the last of the Chinese take out food she had picked up on her way over to his place. After they finished eating, and had cleared the table, they put the empty containers into the garbage. Finished with that, they went into Frank's small living room. The picture of Miriam was no longer in sight. It had been put away, finally. Frank had made up his mind. It had been time to forget the past and start in a new direction with a new lady in his life.

She asked him, "So how's your chess case coming along?"

Frank was sitting along side her on his sagging couch. From his shirt pocket he retrieved a folded piece of paper. "Here's a list of the remaining players who were involved in the final tournament."

He handed her the list of names that Andy Tatum had given him. Cary Ann read the names to herself. Then with her head canted toward the left side, you could see the wheels turning in her mind, as if she was mentally putting something together. Meanwhile Frank had gotten up and gone to the kitchen while she read the list over again.

"Frank," she called out to him. "These names don't make any sense." Her eyes sparkled with a discovery. He came back with two glasses of wine and put them down on the coffee table in front of her. He sat down next to her, took the list and looked at it again.

152

"What doesn't make sense? It's just a list of names." He said as he handed the list back to her.

"As I remember it, the first bunch of names you gave me the first initial of the last names spelled CHEQUE as in CHECK mate, correct?"

"Sure."

"Well then shouldn't some of the last names spell MATE, as in CHECK MATE."

"I would think so, why?" His mind tuning into her new avenue of thought.

"These don't do that."

Frank looked at the list as she held it up for him. She was right. The names on this list spelled MAE. "How could that be? Something is wrong, what have I missed?" He thought it didn't have to spell MATE, but he figured it would.

"God, maybe you should be a detective."

"Thank you, but no thanks. I don't like getting shot at."

MARTIN

He was in luck. Rick's boat was moored at the back of the marina on "Q" dock. Also the Snoqualmie River was flowing so heavy with winter rain runoff that the fresh river water had inundated deep back into the marina as well. The weather in Everett had been so cold these last few days that the surface of the water in the back of the marina had frozen solid.

The ice was about four inches thick in most of the area and foot prints in the loose snow that had fallen last night covering the ice revealed that several boaters had begun taking short cuts across the ice to the gate that was supposed to keep anyone other than owners out of the area. They took this shortcut rather than walk clear down to the end of the walk and then to the gate and out to the parking lot. Perhaps it provided them with more of a thrill of the daring walk on the ice rather than actually saving them time.

Rick was someone who spent almost all his spare time on board his boat, which seemed to be quite a bit of time. Not quite a live-a-board, but nearly so. As a rule he arrived at the boat about seven o'clock each evening when he could come.

He'd made a point of arriving ahead of Rick. He needed the time to make his preparations. He'd climbed onto Rick's boat from the dock, then after surveying the situation he went aft and let himself slip over the side of the boat to the ice.

The freeboard of the boat was just high enough so that when he let go of the rail, he fell almost a foot or slightly more to the icy surface. Gratefully he hit the ice with a solid thump. He took the time to look around the area carefully being sure that he was totally alone.

In the back pack that he had brought along, he pulled out a large old fashioned auger hand drill and a large, but coarse wood bit. He slowly drilled holes through the ice, each hole as close to the previous hole as possible, sometimes breaking the small barrier out between the two adjoining holes. He did this completely around the area where he had landed getting off the boat.

He put the auger and the wood bit back in his back pack, then he brushed the dry snow over the holes until they could not be seen, leaving the appearance that the ice seemed solid over the entire area. Then he walked away, crossing the ice toward the shelter of a covered power boat moorage on the adjoining dock right behind Rick's boat.

He waited patiently, standing under the roof of the nearby powerboat shed. The covered moorage, designed to keep the weather off the boats, was also keeping some of it off him. He was shivering with the cold when Rick got to the boat. When he saw Rick arrive and go aboard the boat, he left his place of shelter from under the roof and walked across the ice to the back of the boat. He knocked on the stern quarter of the hull. Rick, who still had his coat on, came topside and looked down.

"My gosh, how are ya?"

"I'm fine thanks." Without waiting he went on, "Say, I've got a problem. I made dinner reservations for four people at the Marina restaurant, but my partner couldn't make it. Now I've got two ladies for dinner and need someone to spend the evening with one of them."

"Are you inviting me to dinner?" he asked hopefully. He was hungry and not wanting to cook.

"That's it, and I'll pick up the tab."

"Actually, I welcome the invitation. I just got in and I was wondering what I'd do for dinner."

"Great! Come on then, let's do it."

"Just the way I am?"

"Absolutely."

Rick turned around locked his sliding hatch and started to go forward to get off the boat. He heard his friend call to him, "Hey come on, you can go this way."

"Uhh. . . . Yeah, all right." He returned to the back of the boat and saw his friend standing on the ice.

He hesitated only briefly and climbed up on the gunwale, letting himself fall to the surface. Just as he hit, he felt the ice give way from under him and the cold enveloped him immediately. He fought the cold darkness, but only briefly. His strength ebbed so fast he didn't stand a chance.

The Game Resumes

R			Q	K	B	N	R
P	P	P			P	P	
			P				P
				N			
		B		*P*		B	
		N	*P*		*P*		
P	*P*	*P*				*P*	*P*
R		*B*	*Q*	*K*			*R*

KBP-KB3

THIRD MONDAY IN JANUARY

Frank dressed slowly despite the cold in the morning air which was causing goose bumps all over his body. Then he went into the bathroom and closed the bathroom window while he shaved to stop the draft from blowing in on him. When he finished shaving, he went to the kitchen where he poured a bowl full of cold cereal and covered it with milk from the refrigerator. As he started to eat his cereal, he opened the morning paper reading it slowly, as was his usual manner. When he got to the personals, he saw the last chess move listed plus a new one.

6. ------------ N-K4XN
7. KBP-KB3 ----

"Oh no, not again!" His mind went blank with worry.

OFFICE
Sitting at his desk with his legs perched up across the corner of his desk, Frank scanned the morning reports. There were the usual highway accidents, domestic situations and a couple of robberies. But he didn't find anything that looked like the type of incident he was expecting to find listed. He was glad that he hadn't found what he expected, but he was uneasy about it as well.

Later in the morning after he had finished his routine office paperwork and monthly reports to the chief, he asked Jim, "Any thing I can help you with?"

"No. I'm just finishing some of my over due reports. Then I'm gonna stop by my place for lunch and to see if Janet's in a better mood."

"Things any better at home lately?"

"No. In fact just between the two of us, I think she's considering moving out."

"What makes you think that?"

"You know. Little things like phone calls to girl friends that get quiet when I come into the room. The other day I found one of those magazines listing rentals in our garbage as I took it out."

"Sorry, Jim."

160

"Me too. I think I'm too possessive. Or at least she thinks so. When I ask who was on the phone she gets defensive as if it's a big deal that I asked. I only ask because I'm curious. She seems to need more freedom."

"Your curiosity could be a work habit that carry's over from the office."

"I suppose it could be."

Frank picked up his jacket, then he left the office. He knew now where Rick Martin could be located and the address of Fred Andrews as well. He was going to try to talk with these two men today, then he would attempt to locate Harvey Eldridge, the final player in the millionaires chess game.

He had driven east out of the city on the old highway and when he crossed the old two lane bridge he began to look for the road he needed. He almost passed it before he saw it and had to brake quickly to make the turn off. The car behind him screeched its brakes to keep from hitting him and sounded their horn as they went by in the other lane.

An almost invisible dirt and gravel path of a road led him through scrub trees and tall grass on both sides. Frank couldn't see anything in any direction from his position on the road with the exception of the road in front of him and behind him. He found Mr. Martin's old family farm just off the Snoqualmie River and stopped in the open area near a large old barn that seemed as if it was ready to fall down at anytime, or with the next passing storm. One of the farm hands met him near the barn after he'd stopped his car.

161

He rolled the car window down. "Mr. Martin around?" He asked from inside the car.

The man now standing at Frank's car window looked him over carefully while he maneuvered a toothpick from one side of his mouth to the other. Then, when he was satisfied about Frank, he told him, "Mr. Martin went down to his boat a few days ago, an he ain't come back yet."

"Is it unusual for him to be gone for long stretches without a word from him?"

"Yes, Sir. This is pretty much the way he's always been. He ain't needed here ta run the place. Me'n the other fella's take care of things. Not much to do around here this time of year."

When Frank arrived at the Everett marina, he found a visitor parking place just outside the marina office door. Once he had walked up the heavy wooden steps and was inside the warm office he asked the young woman at the reception desk, "I need to know a dock number where Rick Martin's boat is moored."

Without hesitation, she said, "I'm sorry. I'm not allowed to give out that information."

Needing an answer he said, "I'll need to speak to the port manager then."

The young woman rose from her desk and walked toward a closed door behind her. She knocked lightly then opened the door and poked her head inside and spoke softly. Moments later a middle aged man appeared, and he, too, told Frank that it was against

162

Port policy to divulge that information. After producing his identity and badge for the port manager, the manager agreed to take him to Mr. Martin's boat, but only because he was with the police department.

They drove up the parking lot in a Port of Everett pickup truck and parked near the rest rooms. The manager led the way and cautioned Frank about the ice in the area. The ice on the walk itself had been disposed of with a white chemical agent that melted the ice. Frank wondered if it contaminated the water as well. They walked down the "Q" dock until they reached a dark green sail boat.

"This is it," the port manager said as he pointed to the boat.

"Can we go aboard the boat and see if he's here?" Frank asked.

"Sure." The port manager then climbed aboard and Frank followed him. They worked their way around some fenders laying on the deck until they reached the main hatch.

"He's not here."

"How do you know?"

"The hatch is locked from the outside."

As they turned around to start forward again, the manager happened to look down and made the remark. "Looks like something went through the ice here."

Frank felt a rumbling in his stomach as he looked down at the apparent hole in the ice. Though there was new ice filling the hole, it did seem as though something, or someone had gone through the ice. He moved to the edge of the boat knowing there was no use putting off what he had to do.

"Any way down there from here?" he asked.

The port manager looked around, then spied what he was looking for and said, "Yeah, there's a Jacob's ladder bundled up inside his dinghy on the coach roof here."

"A Jacob's ladder?"

"Yes. Here, I'll show you how it works." Then he pulled the ladder out of the small boat's interior and lowered it over the side of the gunwale toward the frozen surface below. The top supports were clinging to the edge of the boat's upper hull.

Frank, using great caution, began to lower himself one rung at a time down over the edge of the boat. His hands gripped the edge of the boat with tenacity. When he was just low enough to let one of his feet settle on the ice without putting his entire body weight on the ice, he felt it gently with his foot. Once he was satisfied it would hold his full weight, he released his grip on the Jacob's ladder and turned to face the hole.

He gingerly moved to the edge of the hole and knelt down to get a better look. He moved his fingers around the edge of the hole, and he knew most of it was man made. When he looked back up and around him, he saw them more clearly. The foot prints that remained in the light snow were more visible from this level. A shiver ran up his back as he got up and climbed the ladder back up to the boat deck.

"Do you have a diver who can have a look under the ice here?"

The port manager looked at him saying, "You mean now?"

"The sooner the better."

"I can arrange it."

"Do it and get the findings to me ASAP."
He handed the port manager one of his office business cards.

On the drive back to his office he wondered about the coincidence of two of the men who played in the chess match together, also having been in the same marina.

He looked at his watch, "Damn, the day just disappeared." He thought, "I'll have to go see Fred Andrews another day."

JIM'S REPORT

Jim was tired. It had taken him two days to gather and search out the information Frank had asked him to check into. Frank wanted some basic background on his growing list of victims, to see if there was a common link. He'd been to the department of Internal Revenue Service, the department of Motor Vehicles, fifteen neighbors, three private business offices and today he'd even missed lunch. At the end of the day his reports were somewhat slim. Even then he condensed them further for what Frank had wanted.

He scanned them one last time, then put them on Frank's desk.

INVESTIGATIVE INFORMATION REPORT.

Childes, Martin
Real estate broker.
Retired 1981
Tax records indicate wealth of 3.2 million.
Cause of death -- Skull fracture -- Everett marina.
Personal records do not indicate any other ongoing social connection with other listed accidental death victims.

Hanson, Harold
Automobile dealerships.
Semi-retired.
Tax records indicate wealth varies, about $400,000.00 per yr.
Cause of death -- Fell off cliff resulting in a skull fracture. Home on Whidbey Island.
Personal records do not indicate any other ongoing social connection with other listed accidental death victims.

Elders, Clyde
Book dealer, two large stores. Still active in business.
Tax records indicate wealth varies, about $275,000.00
per yr.
Cause of death -- Drowning -- Fell from bridge over
Deception pass. -- Whidbey Island.
Personal records do not indicate any other ongoing
social connection with other listed accidental death
victims.

Jim could have done some of the search work on the
office computer. He had even thought about having
Cary Ann do it for him. He also knew he had handled it
the best way under the circumstances. He felt It had
needed the personal touch, so he had gone to each
location himself.

He leaned back in his chair and rubbed his eyes for a
few seconds relieving some of the drowsiness he was
suffering from. Finally he thought to himself, "Well, I
came in late, I'll have to leave early to make up for it."

He leaned forward, his chair coming level and when
his feet were firmly on the floor he got up. He lifted his
jacket off the back of his chair and slipped his right
arm down into the silky sleeve, the other arm slid into
the other sleeve. He went to the old coat rack that was
behind the open door, lifted his long overcoat off the
hanger he had for it and pulled it on over his jacket. He
had purchased the overcoat when he first made
detective because he wanted to look like a movie
detective. He had since given up that idea. Satisfied
he'd gotten everything done, he left the office.

DIVER REPORT
Frank had returned to headquarters from the courthouse where he'd been testifying in a theft case. As he started walking into the office Mike, the duty sergeant, was on the phone but motioned for him to stop for a second. Frank sat in a chair by his desk and waited. Mike was filling out a report from some information he was getting over the phone. Finished he set the phone on its cradle and turned to Frank.

"Thought I'd better warn you. There's a crew of painters going through the building and I told them they could paint your office this Thursday. That a problem for you guys?"

Frank was well aware of the construction going on in state buildings lately. Even the city library was being moved into a new building. He'd heard their offices were being moved out of this building in the near future. "No. I don't think so. I'll tell Jim but you better tell the night sergeant to tell Don and Kim, okay?"

"Yeah, will do. Actually I'll probably still be here when Don and Kim come in. I'll see they get the word, though."

"Any chance we'll get a say so on the colors?"

"I don't think so."

"It's not gonna be that yucky light green again is it?"

"No, I think it's a light tan, or somethin."

"That it?"

"Yep, see'ya." Mike returned his gaze at more waiting documents on his desk.

Frank finished walking to his office where he found Jim's report on his desk. He knew Jim was a neat individual and he also knew Jim had the ability to find information out about anything faster than anyone in their department. This returned his thinking to the fact that there didn't seem to be any solid connection at this point between the different deaths or the men involved that he could find. Frank was frustrated because he didn't have any solid evidence to warrant spending so much time on his suspicions. Just as he was starting to make some notes for some things he would have Jim check on, the phone rang.

"Frank Chambers here."

"Mr. Chambers, this is Puget Salvage Co."

"Yes, what can I do for you."

"Mr. Chambers, The manager for the Port of Everett contacted us. He asked that we make a search dive under the ice in the Everett Marina. I understand the dive was for your office?"

"Yes, it is. Did you find anything?" Frank almost dreaded the answer he felt was coming.

"A body. An older man. Probably in his fifties or sixties, I'd guess."

Frank knew this information would be on the police report he would ultimately receive. "Was it anywhere near the hole in the ice?"

"Yessir, it was, and there's a police team on the scene, now, taking care of the situation."

"Would you know if it was a man named Rick Martin?"

"I'm not sure, but that sounds like what I heard."

Frank said, "Thank you for calling, and I appreciate your efforts."

"No problem." Frank could hear the hesitation in the person's voice then, "Where do I send the diving bill?"

Frank gave him the address and the department name. He knew the Chief would have a fit. Although on his last monthly report, Frank had assigned an investigation case number to what he was working on, to date it wasn't an approved case. He was still trying to gather enough information to turn it into a legitimate case.

Frank had given Jim the case number so he could charge the time he was spending on this case to it as well. He'd explained to Jim that if any flack was coming from this time being spent, that he'd take responsibility for it as senior detective. Before Frank left the office he called the newspaper and talked to Jennie about the latest chess move in the newspaper's personals column.

"Jennie, I'd like you to insert a chess move in the personals column for me."

"Okay, what's it gonna be?"

"It is 7. KBP-KB3 ----- QN-QB5XB."

SAILING

Cary Ann and Frank were seated in the lunch room
having coffee together. Frank had been telling Cary
Ann how the case he had now named the "The Chess
Game Case" was coming along. He was also telling
her how each man had died.

"Two of them died of skull fractures, three of them
drowned, possibly a fourth drowning, or at least it's
assumed he drowned cause he fell, or jumped off the
ferry and hasn't been found as yet. There was also a
plane crashing into the sound. All of these were
reported as accidents and they all are separate
circumstances, yet I'm certain they are all related
somehow. I just can't seem to prove they were
somehow tied together"

"Why do you feel they are connected?" Cary Ann knew
Frank was certain in his own mind, but by asking him
questions like this, she knew it would help him. This
way he would voice his opinions, and perhaps put
some pieces together that had been lying dormant.

Frank started going through each of them one by one,
giving her the details as he knew them. When he got
to telling her about the death of Harry Ulman, she
listened as she had to the others, but when he had
finished telling her about his circumstances, she said,

"That's strange."

He stopped. His mind quit scanning the facts, and he
looked at her. "What's strange?"

"The events about this guy, Ulman."

"What's strange about it?" He was wondering what he had missed that seemed so apparent to Cary Ann. "Didn't you say his body was found just below Lowell Point?"

"Yeah, the fisherman had been fishing all day, and the last time he started hauling in his net he found Ulman's body in his net. This all happened about a mile from Ulman's boat, which they found anchored off East point."

Frank could see Cary Ann's mind was sorting facts, finally looking at him she said, "Tell you what, why don't you come sailing with me tomorrow. You do have Saturday off don't you?"

"Well, I can take it off if I like." Surprised he added, "I didn't know you were a sailor. In fact I didn't know you even had a sailboat." In the back of his mind there was a nagging memory trying to surface.

"Lot'sa things you don't know about me yet, and I don't tell many people about my private life."

He knew this was the case because he'd heard one or two things about her around the office. Such as her being a loner, yet you would hear things about most others he worked with. He said, "Okay, what, where and when?"

"Meet me at my boat." She fished in her purse and pulled out a key ring. Slipping a key off a small key ring she handed it to him and smiled, " I'm on 'C' dock south, number twenty seven. This key will get you in the gate and I'll expect to see you at nine thirty, give or take."

"Cary, is it gonna be warm enough to go sailing this time of year?"

"Will be for me, but you might want'a wear extra clothes, like a sweater, or couple of sweat shirts and bring a change of clothes just in case." Cary was already aware the weather man had promised a nice day tomorrow, the first in some time.

At nine the next morning Frank once again found himself at the Everett Marina. He was beginning to think his case was leading him here on purpose. He parked in an area removed from the dock area. He had done this as everything else was marked, No parking, or Reserved or something else he didn't qualify for.

Cary had told him to be sure to do this so his car wouldn't get towed away. He looked around and found a cart in a nearby red brick enclosure. Back at his car he opened the trunk and put his bag of clothes into the cart along with two bottles of white wine and one of white Zinfandel. He also had some good selections of cheese, and some pickle wraps to munch on. He had learned how to make them years earlier from Miriam. Most people he fed them to, always enjoyed them for a snack.

Frank was having difficulty maneuvering the cart through the gate. Its two wheel axle kept hanging up on one corner of the gate. He'd struggled with this until a young strawberry blond girl, about nine years old, came along and held the gate open for him.

"Thanks, Sweetheart," he said as he smiled at her.

"You're welcome, Mr. Chambers," she said after he was through the gate and before she started to walk away.

"Wait," he said. She then turned to face him and he continued, "How'd you know my name?"

"Cary Ann asked me to watch for you." Then she turned and started skipping down the walk away from him. He noticed she was heading toward 'C' walk.

When he got to number twenty seven on "C" walk he recognized the sailboat as the one in the picture on Cary Ann's desk at work. Cary Ann greeted him as she stood by the side of the white sail boat. He could hear the soft splashing of water as it ran from an engine's exhaust system. Cary Ann climbed aboard the boat and had him hand his stuff to her. She put it all down on the starboard cockpit seat. Onboard the boat while he was putting his stuff where she had shown him, in what she called the quarter berth, Cary Ann took his cart back to the end of the main dock where some other boater could use it. Finished, Frank went back up to the cockpit of the boat where he met Cary Ann just getting back.

"Cary, I'm pretty new to sailing. I've been out with some of the fella's a couple a times on a motor boat, but never on a sailboat."

"No problem, I'll show you what and how to do everything until you catch on. To start with," she was now standing up on the small side deck of the boat, "Come up here and use this boat hook to hold us in place along side the dock." A little nervous, he did as he was told. He also wrapped one arm around the lower shroud to support himself. He wasn't used to taking orders from a woman, but somehow with Cary Ann it seemed to be a comfortable feeling.

Cary had gotten off the boat, cast the bow line loose, then the stern mooring lines. When she had finished, she climbed back aboard. Once she had the life lines hooked back in place, she had him slip the boat hook loose from the cleat on the dock. As he moved carefully back toward the cockpit of the boat and sat down on the starboard cockpit seat, he marveled at how well she handled the boat. It seemed as if it required little effort on her part.

After they'd cleared the harbor, and the mouth of the river running past it, she had him hold the helm for her as she raised the sails. He had been nervous, but she'd given him instructions as they went along so it worked out okay for both of them. The wind had been coming over the left side of the boat, she informed him that it was the port side and they sailed at an angle that made him nervous at first as the boat heeled slightly. Cary settled the boat on a course, then she had him take the helm again and he began to relax more. Now it excited him to feel the power of the boat under his feet. He began to understand it would stay upright.

About three and a half or four hours later, they arrived off East point, and Cary Ann had started the boat's engine so Frank could keep the boat headed into the breeze while she took the sails down. She folded the mainsail on top of the main boom and covered it with the sail cover. Having finished putting the sails away, now they were moving under power. After they motored a short distance, Cary Ann took the engine out of gear letting the boat drift with the slight tidal current, she got a chart out and had laid it on a cockpit seat next to Frank. She was using it to explain her ideas about the circumstances surrounding Harry Ulman's death.

"You see, Frank, his boat was found anchored right about here, right?" She said as she suggested a point on the chart with her finger nail covered with pink finger nail polish.

It took him a few seconds to orient himself with where she was pointing on the nautical chart, and where that was in relationship to a point on the nearby land. Once he had it all placed in his mind he said, "That's what I understand from the reports."

"Okay, and his body was found about a mile that way." Cary Ann's arm came up and her fingers were pointing in the direction she wanted him to look.

He looked to where she was pointing, then looked at her chart and nodding, said, "Yep."

She paused a moment, then continued, "Well look around you, what do you see?"

"Water. Lots of water."

"Okay, but if you think about it, and look around to the north and the south, you'll see that the main body of the water goes back and forth in those directions. And when the tide changes, sometimes it moves pretty fast through here."

"What're you telling me?"

"I'm telling you his body couldn't get from here," she was pointing to the chart, "to here," again pointing at the chart.

"Why couldn't it?"

"Because the tidal current would have swept it up there, or down there." She said, pointing up to the north west and then down to the south east. "It couldn't go across current to that location over there where the fisherman pulled him up in his net."

"Well, I'll be damned. . . . So somebody put him over there."

"Or he was put overboard over there and someone anchored his boat over here afterwards."

When Cary Ann was satisfied Frank was aware of the effects that mother nature had on the area they were in, they got under way again. They motored under power to the marina at Langley, where Cary Ann had called ahead on her VHF radio making arrangements with the harbor master for a guest berth with an electrical hook up for the night.

Frank had gotten off the boat when Cary Ann pulled the boat along side the guest dock and he held the boat in place with a line looped around a middle dock cleat until she could come ashore with him to finish securing the boat to the dock.

Below deck and in the nice warm cabin they dined on a one pot meal that Cary had put together. Then they ate the pickle wraps Frank had brought along, which Cary Ann found delicious. Frank explained to her how they were made up of cream cheese with a dill pickle wrapped in thin slices of ham. The wine had made them both a little giddy.

Later in the evening after they had crawled up into the vee berth and fallen asleep, he was suddenly awakened by Cary Ann climbing out of bed. He could hear the wind howling in the rigging outside.

"What's up?"

"Gonna check our mooring lines to be sure we're still snug."

He watched her walk aft, and her nudity seemed natural for her.

"You'll get cold."

"You'll get me warm." Then she disappeared out the hatch, the cold rushing in.

When she returned to the cabin, she was cold. *'Icy'* Frank thought, but she snuggled up to his back her nipples hard against him and she was soon fast asleep as if nothing had ever taken place. He lay awake listening to the weather, thinking about what he had learned that afternoon. No doubt in his mind any longer. Harry Ulman had been murdered.

What's Going on?

R			Q	K	B	N	R
P	P	P			P	P	
		P					P
		N		$\mathcal{P}$		B	
		$\mathcal{N}$	$\mathcal{P}$		$\mathcal{P}$		
$\mathcal{P}$	$\mathcal{P}$	$\mathcal{P}$				$\mathcal{P}$	$\mathcal{P}$
$\mathcal{R}$		$\mathcal{B}$	$\mathcal{Q}$	$\mathcal{K}$			$\mathcal{R}$

QN-QB5XB

FOURTH SATURDAY OF JANUARY

He hadn't really been expecting another counter move to the chess game, but he picked up a copy of the morning paper at a nearby vending machine on his way back to the small cabin he was now inhabiting. He'd been lucky to have come across the owner of the cabin quite by accident. He had been in the local Mom and Pop grocery store where he had stopped for a cold soda. He'd been looking over the local bulletin board when a voice behind him asked, "Can I help yah find somethin?"

He turned to see the store's owner, an older man, looking in his direction. "Well, I'm just visiting for a short time and kinda like the area. Now I'm considering spending a few months, so I was looking to see if there were any places for rent around here."

The man seemed to be checking his feelings, then he said, " Fact is I've got a small place down on the edge of the water that's empty most of the time anymore."

"You interested in renting it on an open rental basis?"

The old man had already decided, now he leaned over, got a piece of scratch paper from under the counter and began to draw a small map. Then he opened his cash register drawer and pulled a key out of one of the change containers. He handed him the key right then saying,

"It's too old to hurt, your bein' there'd dry it out some. Probly be good fer the place." They'd come to an agreement on a fee for the rental and he'd moved his stuff in right after he'd left the store.

After he had returned to the small cabin with the daily paper, he'd started a fire in the small heating stove with drift wood he'd come across on the beach and some windfall wood along the edge of the tree line nearby. He'd cut these small pieces of wood up to a size he could use in the stove. He did this with a small hand held brush saw he'd gotten at the local hardware store. He had placed a kettle of water on the stove to heat. After the water had gotten hot, he made a cup of tea and now sitting with his cup of tea, he opened the paper and read it slowly for any news relating to any accident victims. As he scanned down the list of personal advertisements, he saw what he had feared. There it was.

7. KBP-KB3 ------ QN-QB5XB

He could feel the hair rise on the back of his neck. Previously he had set up the game of chess he had been playing on a portable chess board he'd brought along. He got up from the small scarred kitchen table and moved to the chess board on a table near the front window of the cabin, made the move that had been in the paper and sat back staring at the game.

Fear was beginning to rise again. "What's going on?" He was thinking, "Is somebody onto me?"

Had he made an error? He knew the flight dock attendant had gotten a good look at him near Jacques' plane, but he felt he covered that encounter over by pretending to be an aircraft mechanic. Nobody had been around for Harry, he knew that for a fact. He couldn't be sure about Rick, but thought he had gone unseen.

LICENSE PLATE

Frank had arrived at the office early. The drive into work had been through blustery weather. There was only a light rain, the kind that is persistent and soaks things thoroughly, but the wind was howling. Bits of scrap paper and debris was swirling through the air, especially on all the cross streets. On some of the streets as he crossed through an intersection he could feel the car being buffeted by the wind. He was glad to have a protected parking area, even though the wind sucked the air rapidly through the parking area, it was fairly dry. He rode the elevator up to his floor and was surprised to find Jim already at his desk.

"Morning, Jim, kinda early aren't yah?"

"I figured I'd turn over a new leaf."

"Really."

"Truth is, Janet asked me to leave early today."

"The heck she did?"

"Yes, she's moving today and didn't want me around to make things difficult."

"I'm sorry, partner. I know how you feel about this."

"Yes, well at least It's a peaceful parting but I'll miss her being around the place." Then he changed the subject as if to avoid the pain of her leaving.

"Hey, before I forget it, those pictures from the Whidbey Island police department finally came in late yesterday. I think you might find them interesting. "

He pushed his chair back away from his desk, pulled open the center drawer and reached into the drawer. His hand came out with a small white envelope and he pulled the flap open.

He took out several pictures saying, "It looks like some of the roll was ruined and the full roll of film hadn't been exposed."

He handed Frank the copies of all the pictures they had received. Frank settled into his chair, turned on the small lamp on the left corner of his desk, spread the pictures out on top of his desk and looked at them slowly. One of them was a photo of Lopez Island in the distance and one of the distant southern shore line well beyond Port Angeles. Both pictures had the entrance to Deception Pass in them, but it was easy to see the subject matter was different and was intended to be.

The one picture that caught his attention was the one taken at an odd angle of the bridge. The picture also captured the image of two cars on what appeared to be the south end of the bridge. The other pictures were of no help. When he finally looked up, he saw Jim smiling at him.

He said to Jim, "What?"

"That picture. The picture of the two cars was probably taken by accident as the guy fell off the bridge."

"Or, as he was pushed off the bridge as the case may be."

"Look at it again." Jim insisted, still grinning.

Frank looked at the one picture again, but couldn't pick out what it was that Jim was expecting him to see. He looked up at Jim questioningly.

"Look closely. I think you can see the front end of both cars and there are license plates showing on both cars."

Frank looked again. He studied the photo carefully. "You may be right, but you can't see them well enough to do any good with the numbers."

"I've got a friend in Seattle in the crime photography unit. I was thinking I'd ask her to do a blow up of those plates to see if we can get the numbers off them."

"If it can be done, I'd say give it a go and try it." He stacked the pictures back into a pile and handed them back to Jim.

"I'll take them by her place today at lunch time but we may need the negatives."

"If you do, call Bob Powers at the Whidbey Island police department, he'll have the negatives. You might offer him copies of any blown up photos you get as well."

"Will do." He said as he reached over for Frank's Rolodex and found the number for Bob Powers.

Frank picked up the report from the black plastic basket on the top of his right desk corner. He'd been expecting this report. He had asked for all accidental death reports to be sent to him as soon as they came in. He no longer wanted to wait for the standard daily reports.

- -

Accidental Death Report Form.

VICTIMS NAME ---- Rick Martin --

CAUSE OF DEATH -- Drowning / exposure –

TIME OF DEATH --- Time hard to fix due to body temperature.

CIRCUMSTANCES --- Appears to have jumped from rear of boat onto the ice, which broke under his weight. The affect of hypothermia and the lack of air under the ice, caused his death.

Form # 010692-93

- -

NEWSPAPER

The phone began to ring just after lunch. Frank had been in Cary Ann's office where they had just arranged for an evening together and he was returning to his own office. He rushed through the door to pick up the receiver .

"Frank Chambers here."

"Mr. Chambers this is Jennie at the newspaper office."

"Yes, Jennie, what's up?"

"I had a curious phone call routed to me a few minutes ago. A man called and asked who was making the counter chess moves to the ongoing chess game that had been in the newspaper."

"Wha'd you tell him?"

"Well, at first I played like I didn't understand, but he took the time to explain what he was talking about. I made him wait as if I were looking through files, then I said that I didn't know, that there wasn't anything to show who either person was but I'd try to find out. I asked if he'd give me his name and phone number, and that I'd call him back with the info when I had it."

"Nice try Jennie, what happened?"

"He said, no thanks, he was just curious about the game."

"Did he sound just curious, or seeking some information about me?"

186

"No, I don't think he was just curious. I think he was actually wanting to know who was really making the other moves." After some hesitation, she added, "If he calls again what should I tell him?"

Frank thought about it for a few moments then said, "I'll give you a name and a phone number, but don't give it to anyone else other than him, okay."

"Okay. . . .Why?"

"It's my personal number and a name I've made up, an I don't wanna start gettin crank calls."

"Gotcha. I'll tell him I was able to find out who one of the players is and make your number available."

"Sounds good, Jennie, and thanks."

FIRST SATURDAY IN FEBRUARY

Frank had been up early enough to take the paper out of the paper boys hand when he approached Frank's door in the hallway. "Thanks," Frank said as the boy gave him the paper.

"You're welcome, Mr. Chambers." It was a real surprise for the paper boy, because hadn't seen Frank in better than a year. Frank always left the check for the paper boy with the apartment manager, and the check always contained more than Frank owed him.

Frank had already been up long enough that he had finished his breakfast and even washed his dishes. He hadn't dried them, but he rarely did. Most of the time he just let them air dry in the dish drainer. After he got the paper, he stood in his kitchen doorway leaning against the frame, the kitchen light leaving a slight shadow on the newspaper page he was reading. He had gone right to the personal ads.

"Thank God!" he said to no one as he finished reading the ads. He was relieved there wasn't another chess move in the paper this morning. He had been expecting another chess move, even though he had made a counter opposing move to the last one appearing in the newspaper. Now he could only hope he would get a phone call from the opposing player, hopefully asking to play a game against him personally.

JIM'S REPORT

Jim finally finished typing out the latest information Frank had asked him for, and he was going to leave the typed copy on Frank's desk before he left. He also left a sticky paste-it note attached to the top of the report, saying, "Frank, I'm afraid this is pretty much run of the mill information except for one of them."

PERSONAL INFORMATION REPORT.

Quine, Jacques
*Owned a small airport and air charter service.
* He was still active in the business.
*Tax records indicate wealth varies, about $375,000.00 per yr.
 *Cause of death -- Assumed air crash into Puget Sound.
 *Personal records do not indicate any other ongoing social connection with the other listed accidental death victims.

Ulman, Harry
* Banking industry.
* Retired.
 *Tax records indicate wealth about $210,000.00 per year.
 *Cause of death -- Fell over board and drowned, private yacht.
*Personal records do not indicate any other ongoing social connection with the other listed accidental death victims.

Evans, Richard
* Land developer.
 *Still active in business
 *Tax records indicate wealth varies, averages about
$325,000.00 per yr. His bank records indicate recent
large cash withdrawal.
*Cause of death -- Apparently fell over board, from the
 Mukilteo ferry, assumed to be a drowning victim.
* Personal records do not indicate any other ongoing
social connection with the other listed accidental death
victims.
*Note: Investigated business records. This action
taken after speaking with bank about large withdrawal.
Business records show some discrepancy in business
dealings as of late. Could have been in great financial
stress.

Martin, Rick
*Farming, large scale enterprise.
*Semi-retired.
*Tax records indicate wealth varies, about
$380,000.00 per yr.
*Cause of death -- Hypothermia, fell through ice in
marina and drowned. Personal records do not indicate
any other ongoing social connection with other listed
accidental death victims.

- -

LICENSE NUMBER

Jim had gotten in touch with his friend about the photographs of the cars taken on the south end of the bridge over Deception Pass. She had carefully blown them up as far as she could without complete distortion. The pictures were useable for his needs, but only with a magnifying glass. Back at the office he and Frank had spent several minutes peering at the photos, and they finally agreed on what the license plate numbers and letters were.

Jim immediately checked with the department of motor vehicles to get the name and address of the registered owner. One of them belonged to Clyde Elders, and now they had a name and address of the owner of the other automobile. They were glad that things were beginning to look favorable for a change. Any lead was welcome.

CAR'S OWNER

They didn't want to tip him off that they were going to visit him, so it had been decided to visit Ralph Sawyer on Saturday morning. They arrived just after ten in the morning and parked their unmarked car in front of the small house. The house was located in a small cull-de-sac in one of the newer housing developments in the area north of town. Frank knocked on the door and waited, Jim stood on the other side of the doorway. A small child, who apparently had recently decided to take it upon himself to be the one who answered the door, opened the door without hesitation. Looking up, he smiled, turned and ran back into the house. "Daddy, there's some men at the door."

With the door still standing open Frank and Jim could see a man in his late twenties coming toward them. "Mornin', can I help you?"

Frank took out his identification and said, "Mr. Sawyer, I'm Frank Chambers, this is my partner Jim Parsons."

Ralph Sawyer looked confused. "So?"

"We'd like to talk to you about your car, ummm . . . " Frank checked his notes, "A nineteen seventy three Volvo."

Still confused, Ralph said, "I don't have that car anymore, I sold it about the middle of November."

Frank, surprised but undaunted said, "It's still registered in your name, Mr. Sawyer."

"The hell it is."

"Yes, it is."

"Can't help you there. I signed the pink slip off to the fella that bought if from me. Was it in an accident or somethin?"

"Or something," Frank came back with, then continued, "Who'd you sell it to?"

"Come on in, I'll see if I can find the guy's name."

They followed him into a house that definitely showed signs of being lived in. It was much too warm, probably to keep the children warm, not knowing it was more harmful to their health. Ralph was rummaging through a bunch of papers piled on top of an old table pushed against one wall, when his wife came into the room and said, "What're you looking for honey?"

"That guys name who bought our old Volvo."

"Oh, I probly threw that stuff out. I didn't think we'd need it anymore."

He turned to Frank and held his hands out palms up in dismay, his face in a grimacing twist. "Sorry, but I think his name was Holman, or Hammon, something like that."

"How is it he came to you for a car?"

"I had an ad in the paper listing it for sale and a phone number. " Frank made a note of this information.
"Did he give you a check for the car?"

"No, he paid me in cash for it."

"What did he look like?"

"Umm . . . Tall, kinda slender, dark hair." ...

"Black hair," his wife interjected.

"A. . . .yeah, and he had a bald spot on the top of his head in the back, you know up here." He said pointing to the top of his head. "Wearing jeans and a sweat shirt as I recall. Mmmm . . . late forties or so, maybe more."

"He seemed polite," his wife added again.

"What color is the car?"

"Dark green, or was anyway."

"Thank you, Mr. Sawyer. You got anything Jim?"

"Nope. Not much else we can find out here at the time."

"Mr. Sawyer, we'll let ourselves out. Oh, if you see the car again, or if you think of something else that might help us would you call me?"

"Yessir." Frank handed him one of his departmental cards as they began to leave.

CARY ANN'S

Cary Ann had fixed Frank a Mesquite Chicken dinner, and he had eaten it heartily. It wasn't that he was that hungry, just that it wasn't a flavor of chicken he'd had before and it was delicious. After dinner, he helped her with the dinner dishes. He dried them while she washed. She found it odd for a man to dry dishes, but she was glad he had this kind of nature. When they were finished, she said,

"Lets see how your chess game is, Frank."

"You wanta play a game of chess?" He knew she could play, but this surprised him. In fact, lots of things about her were surprising him.

"Sure. You get us a glass of wine, I'll get a chess set out and meet you in the living room. Frank smiled, then turned to find a couple of wine glasses in the cupboard. He set the glasses down on the drain board near the refrigerator and opened the refrigerator door. He found the bottle lying on a bottom shelf. After pouring the wine and replacing the bottle, he walked into the living room where he saw Cary Ann setting the chess game up on the glass top coffee table. He put the glasses on the table and then he sat on the couch. Cary Ann sat in a stuffed chair opposite him. She picked up her glass of blush wine and settled back into the depth of the chair waiting for Frank to make the first move.

Frank opened with the Queen's gambit by moving the Queen's Pawn to the Queen's four square. Cary Ann took her time as she leaned over to make her chess move. Frank's eyes enjoyed her cleavage as she did so. Cary Ann enjoyed his gaze, and she had made it easy for him to look at her on purpose. She countered his chess move easily with her Kings Knight to Kings Bishop Three. He soon found he hadn't taken her game seriously enough and she soon beat him badly.

"I'm sorry, Frank." She had declined the offered Queen's Bishop Pawn, and was now apologizing for walking all over him during the game. Once she had his game in trouble, he hadn't been able to recover.

"No problem. You're a better player than I expected."

"He began setting up the board again. This time white was on the other side of the board giving Cary Ann the first move. This time he won, but barely. He'd found he couldn't make any error in his game with her, because she would pounce on it, winning an advantage. When that game was finished, Cary Ann said, "Why don't you show me the game your assumed killer is playing in the newspaper."

Quickly Frank set up the chess board, turned to reach over behind him, where he pulled his jacket off the end corner of the couch, then he reached into his inside jacket pocket, pulling out a small sheet of folded paper. Once he was settled down at the board again, he moved the pieces one by one explaining to her as he went about the outcome of the game he had expected.

"You see, if I had played this game the way the original game had been played, and the way most players would have played it, the game would be over by now."

She looked at the chess board a few moments, as if she had missed something. "Is that all?"

"Well, yeah." Not understanding why she couldn't see the end of the game.

"What about the rest of the moves?"

"There wouldn't be any more moves. The game would be over."

"How many moves to this point?" She asked.

Frank looked at the board and counted the moves, " Umm. There, there, over here, then there, that one,"

Finally, he said, "Eight moves."

"And how many men on your list?"

He looked up in surprise, his mind kicking into over drive and said, " Ten." He looked at the board again, understanding her meaning now. "What's going on?"

Cary Ann, sensing his thinking, said, "Doesn't make sense does it?"

"No, the game would be over before all the men on the list of players were dead." He thought about it some more, then, "It has to be tied in somehow! It has to be!"

A Sacrifice?

R			Q	K	B	N	R
P	P	P			P	P	
			P				P
						B	
		N		*P*		B	
		N	*P*		*P*		
P	*P*	*P*				*P*	*P*
R			*Q*	*K*			*R*

QB-KN5

FIRST SATURDAY IN MARCH

Frank had fussed most of the morning. He wanted to make the call earlier, but hadn't wanted to wake Andrew Tatum up. Now it was after ten in the morning so he dialed the number. It rang three times before the housekeeper picked it up.

"Si."

He recognized her voice right away. "Porfavor, Senior Tatum?"

"Si. Un momento."

He heard her put the phone down on a table. The wait seemed to be much longer than it really was. "Hello."

"Mr. Tatum, this is Frank Chambers. We spoke recently."

"Oh, sure. What can I do for you, Mr. Chambers?"

"Actually, I wanted to know if you were all right."

"I'm fine, why?"

"I was concerned because there was another chess move in the paper and I wanted to check to see if you were okay."

"No problem. I'm fine . . . really."

"You haven't noticed anyone around lately that would make you suspicious?"

"Well, I don't look over my shoulder all the time, but no, I haven't noticed anyone unusual around."

"Good ... Good. Say, Mr. Tatum would you mind if I drop by one evening soon? I'd like to discuss something curious that I've come across recently." He was thinking about the chess game in the paper and the amount of moves it contained.

"No, not at all. Any time you like."

"Thank you, Sir. I'll call first."

"No need, just come by."

Frank hung up the phone and looked once again at the new move in the newspaper.

7. --------------- QN-QB5XB
8. QB-KN5 --------

This latest move in the newspaper, Queen's Bishop to King Knight's five, threatened to capture his Queen. What seemed strange was that this chess move had appeared in the paper, but as yet he hadn't found any new deaths that he could attribute to his killer.

Frank mulled it over for most of the remaining morning, then he called Jennie at the newspaper and gave her his next move. It was the move he felt was the correct one to use as an answering move.

It was 8. QB-KN5 -------- QBXKBP

VOLVO

Jim had been waiting patiently for Frank to get back from his coffee break. He'd noticed that Frank's coffee breaks had gotten longer now that he and Cary Ann had become close. When Frank finally came back, he was smiling, something Frank hadn't done much of before he had become involved with Cary Ann. Jim was thinking, *'She's good for him.'*

"Frank, I've gotten some interesting news and I think we should take a ride to check it out."

"Good news, I hope?"

"I don't know, could go either way. You remember I had the registration flagged at motor vehicles and we had our patrol cars keeping a lookout for that Volvo that Mr. Sawyer sold to an unknown party."

"Yeah. Somebody find it?"

"Yes. The Motor Vehicle Department called. A change of ownership came through yesterday on it."

"Good. Let's go talk to the owner."

"The Volvo's in a wrecking yard Frank."

"Oh no."

"Well, it may not be a complete loss. I think we should go see these people anyway."

"Yeah, could be you're right, let's go."

They got their jackets from the coat rack, slipped them on, and started out of their office. On their way down the hallway Frank watched Jim buttoning his jacket. Frank left his open, and was thinking how Jim's desk was always nice and neat, and that Jim dressed so impeccably.

As they walked by the duty Sergeant's desk, Jim told Sergeant Brown, "Mike, Frank and I are gonna be out at a wrecking yard in Oak Harbor. You can call us on the radio if you need us."

"You got it." He appreciated them letting him know where they could be found.

The drive to Oak Harbor had taken them just slightly over an hour. When they arrived at their destination, they parked in front of the wrecking yard office. Its parking lot was well saturated with oil from many years of leaking engines, transmissions, rear ends, and who knows what else. Nearly everyone who stopped here needed parts of some kind for repair. Jim and Frank walked inside and found the parts counter was in need of an oil change as well. Neither of them leaned on it. The man behind the counter came over wiping his hands on a red oily rag. It too, needed to be changed.

"Yeah, what'cha needin?"

Jim beat Frank to the draw showing his identification to the man, and said, "We need some information about a car you just purchased."

The guy behind the counter looked a little nervous now. He started to turn away, saying, "Wouldn't be me. Hang on jus'a minute." He walked over to a side

202

door of the office. It was dark brown and black from years of greasy hands pushing it open. It opened into the back lot and he hollered out, "Hey Butch, better git your butt in here."

A big man, who was much heavier than was healthy, finally sauntered through the door. He too, was wiping his hands on an old rag. "What?"

"These guys er needin some stuff about a car we just got."

"Which'en?"

Jim explained to him about the Volvo they were looking for. When he was done Butch went over to a metal file cabinet pushed into a far corner, pulled a drawer out, and began looking through a list in one of the files. He said,

"Yep, we had it."

"What do you mean you had it?" Jim said.

"Sent it to the crusher two days ago."

"You mean it's a big heavy metal square somewhere now?" Frank asked, disappointed.

"That's about it." Butch pulled an owner's certificate out of a file in the cabinet and placed it on the counter in front of them. The signature on the certificate said, 'RALPH SAWYER.'

"Did he sign this while he was here?"

"Yep, right over there." He indicated the other end of the counter.

"You actually saw him sign his name to this?"

"Well, he had his one hand holdin the paper, while his other hand was signin it. I couldn't see the pen on the paper, but it looked like he was writin."

"What did this guy look like?" Jim asked.

"Don't rightly remember, but I think he was thin, kinda . . . an, oh yeah, he was a little thin on top. You know losin' his hair back here." He said, pointing to the upper rear part of his own bushy head.

Jim and Frank looked at one another, then Frank said, "Well, thanks, Butch, we appreciate your help. If you remember anything else let us know, okay?"

When they were back out in the unmarked car and as Jim was backing out, Frank said, "Well, it wasn't Sawyer, was it?"

"Nope, but it sounded like the guy he described to us. The one he sold it to."

They drove in silence for a few minutes when Jim asked, "Now what?"

"My guess would be that he bought another car the same way he got that one."

"But why would he sell this one."

"Beats me," Frank said, "There was either a problem

with it or, and I hate this part, he thinks we're onto him. At least he's worried about something." After they had driven in silence for a few moments longer, Frank continued,

"Lets hope he was just having trouble with the car and got rid of it. Because if he thinks we're onto him and he stops now, we may never catch him with what little we have to go on."

A Trade?

R			Q	K	B	N	R
P	P	P			P	P	
			P				P
					B		
		N		*P*			
		N	*P*		B		
P	*P*	*P*				*P*	*P*
R			*Q*	*K*			*R*

QBXKBP

CHESS MOVE

He had driven across the island's narrow and twisted back roads late in the morning to the small local store. He parked in a slot near the far side of the store's lot as if hiding his car, but he wasn't. He put his last three quarters in the slot of the paper box, thinking about how expensive a damn thirty five cent city paper cost out here on the island. He was in luck, as he pulled the door to the paper box and there was just one paper left. . . . the one that filled the display window on the box itself.

With the paper in his hand he wandered over to the nearby local coffee shop. As he entered the door, the waitress recognized him. She knew him as being from the island. She nodded her head to him. A method of acknowledging him, and a good morning all in one motion. She didn't know his name but she had been seeing him around the area lately. "Mornin," she said as she poured him a cup of steaming coffee at an empty seat at the counter before he got to it. Two other men seated nearby nodded good morning to him as well, also without saying anything.

"Mornin all," he said. then he sat down where the coffee cup awaited him. He looked up at the waitress and paused briefly as she put the coffee urn back onto the hot plate nearby. As she turned back to him, he asked, "Could I have a couple of eggs over medium and some toast?"

"Sure can." She then went to the small ordering window to tell the cook what she needed for this customer. "Turn two, and toast it."

Slowly he opened the paper. Trying to be nonchalant and at ease he then turned directly to the personal ads. He had just taken a sip of coffee, and what he saw almost made him spit the coffee out of his mouth. As it was, he swallowed too quickly and the hot coffee burned all the way down.

In the column he read, 8. QB-KN5 --------- QBXKBP

He mulled the chess move over in his mind a few moments then thought, "This bastard is offering me a Queen exchange." It was only a short wait until his breakfast arrived and he ate it hurriedly, unaware the others had noticed his haste in finishing his breakfast. When he finished eating his meal, he dropped some money on the lunch counter that he knew was more than enough to cover the meal. He got up and hurriedly left the shop. He needed to get home to the small rental cabin and to his chess board.

After he had gone out the door, one of the old timers said, "He eats in a mighty big hurry don't he?"

EVENING AT TATUM'S

Frank had called Andrew Tatum's home earlier letting him know he was on his way over. He had also asked Cary Ann if she would like to go along with him and she had jumped at the invitation. They arrived just after seven o'clock. Frank parked near the garage this time as well, but now the garage doors were all closed. They walked to the front door and Frank rang the bell. Shortly the door opened and the house keeper welcomed them in without reservation, she was now feeling more comfortable with Frank's presence.

Andrew was waiting for them in the den. There was an ornate table made from rich dark woods, with chairs to match. The table top was inlaid with several colors of wood, and in the center of the inlay was a chess board set up for a game, with what appeared to be hand carved wooden chess pieces of exotic woods and of the Stanton design, all in place. Nearby a bucket of ice containing a bottle of chilled wine was waiting for their arrival.

"Ahh . . . I see you've brought along a treat for the eyes," he said as Cary Ann entered the room. She turned a slight tinge of pink but enjoyed his approval of her looks.

"Mr. Tatum, this is Cary Ann."

"Please, call me Andrew young lady," he said as he addressed Cary Ann directly. Even in his advanced years he still appreciated the beauty and promise of a woman, age having nothing to do with it.

They sat down around the chess table and Andrew poured them all a glass of a nineteen eighty Reisling.

"Young lady, to your health."

"Thank you," she said.

They carried on a general conversation, but it was obvious that Andrew was taken by Cary Ann. Frank didn't mind.

Finally, Andrew asked, "Tell me, Frank, what is this new development you wanted to speak to me about?"

"Well, recently Cary Ann and I were playing chess together one evening and she made me aware of a discrepancy in my line of thinking."

He went on to explain the game he had been playing against the chess moves that had been showing up in the paper. Finally, he voiced his concern about the amount of moves it presented, also that he couldn't figure out why this particular game opening was being played, and not some other opening that would normally last more than eight moves.

After he had told Andrew his concerns, Andrew asked Frank to tell him about the game he had encountered in the newspaper.

"Oh. Well, I understand the game. I think it's called the Black Death."

A grin showed on Andrew's face. Then, "Ah, you mean it goes like this." He reached out and moved the pieces on the chess set to simulate the opening Frank had named as Frank and Cary Ann looked on.

"Yes, that's it."

"Well, it's not an opening move you'll see very often. Fact is, I've only seen it once in the past several years, myself. It was made popular by Henry Blackburne."

"I've never seen it. Of course, I don't play much chess these days, either."

"Well, I was aware of the opening but had never been exposed to it in a game until a few months ago. It was the winning combination played in our championship match game on the boat last year."

Frank and Cary Ann looked up at him, Frank replying with, "You mean the million dollar game in Nanaimo?"

"One and the same."

OFFICE

"Jim, you know those reports you started putting together for me about the group of chess players that seem to have died accidentally?"

"Yes."

"You got a copy of it handy by any chance?"

"Umm . . . sure," Jim said as he turned to his right, bent over slightly and pulled his bottom desk drawer open. He rifled through a stack of file folders and finally pulled one of them out of the drawer. "Here you are." He handed it across his desk to Frank waiting on the other side.

Frank took several minutes to read through them all again, then he leaned back in his chair placed his hands behind his neck and looked up at the ceiling as if in deep thought.

"Got something?" Jim asked.

"Well. . . .apparently nothing. I've read the file about this guy Evans before, I just couldn't remember who it was for sure."

"Yes, well he was the only one in financial trouble as I recall."

"True, but he's also one of the victims, or at least that's the way it seems to be."

"So, why were you concerned about him?"

"Cary Ann and I were over at Andrew Tatum's the

other night. We were talking about this chess game that's been in the paper and Andrew told me that the opening that's being played through the personal column in the paper, is the same opening that was played in the winning game of their million dollar chess match. Also that it's pretty rare to even see this opening played. Conditions have gotta be just right for it to play out correctly."

"So what's so strange about that?"

"I dunno yet. It just seems odd somehow that the game being played in the paper is the same opening in the tournament as well."

"And Evans was in on it?"

"Yeah. He's the guy that lost the game in the big match and as far as we know he's a corpse at the bottom of the sound somewhere."

"What about the other guy, ahh. . . .What's his name, the guy that won?"

"Harvey Eldridge. Well, I tried calling him, but I haven't been able to reach him yet. Seems he's outta the country right now on an extended vacation cruise somewhere in the Bahamas."

"Do you suppose he's a suspect?"

"Nah, he wasn't around for the last death, or the paper advertised chess move either."

"Do you figure he's safe for the time being?"

213

"Probly, or at least until he gets home. Actually, I'd make bet on the next victim being Fred Andrews."

"Oh yes, which reminds me, I've gotten a lead on him for you. Seems he's pretty much of a recluse. He owns a gold mine somewhere up in the hills, seems he's been home a few days, and he's at home right now. Here's his address."

ANDREWS

Frank arrived at the ferry terminal late, but in time to catch the nine fifteen ferry across from Seattle to Bremerton. His car was located in a position on the inside middle lane, near the end. Not a spot he was particularly fond of. He'd developed a habit of taking something to read with him on these trips across the sound. Frank was not the only one to do this. Taking longer to cross than he liked, he knew this trip usually took almost an hour, sometimes more depending on the weather conditions or tourist traffic.

On this particular morning he didn't even open the book. Instead he elected to explore the upper deck area of the ferry. He walked to the steel stairway leading to the upper deck. At the top of the stairs, when he opened the door leading into the lounge area, he felt the rush of cold air pushing past him into the warmth of the large room. He'd wandered around for longer time than he realized when at the last minute he decided he'd better go to the rest room before the ferry docked.

The men's room was typical of public rest rooms. His nose rejected the smell of urine, "Yuck. When you've got'ta go, you got'ta go." Frank found an empty stall at the end, but latching the door took some effort on his part. He finally got it latched by lifting the door up with his foot slightly. He turned around and pulled some toilet paper off the roll, its built in resistance made the paper tear off in short segments of two or three squares at a time. When he finally had enough he wiped the stainless steel seat off. Pulling his pants and shorts down, he cringed as he sat on the cold seat. Frank hadn't noticed the lack of movement or noise on the ferry.

Suddenly he heard the announcement "Will the owner of the brown four door, with government plate number . . .", He realized it was his car they were talking about. "Damn." He hurried as fast as he dared. Finally almost sliding down the damp steps to the lower deck, where he was met by two deck hands. "This your car buddy?"

"Yeah, sorry, I got stuck in the bathroom."

"I'll need your name and address for my report."

Frank pulled out his police identification and displayed it for him. "Thanks, Mr. Chambers," he said after looking at it. "At least you showed up before we had'a start searchin' the boat."

"You do that if someone doesn't show up like this?"

"Oh yeah. Sometimes it can be an hour or better."

"Why so long?"

"Cause there's so damn many places to look for somebody on this thing, especially if they don't want'a be found."

Frank thought about that as they spoke, then asked, "Couldn't somebody just walk off and leave a car here, without your knowing they had gone?"

"Oh sure. It happens sometimes, you know some old dude drives on the ferry in his car, goes topside an forgets he's got his car with him, an walks off. He catches a cab, gets home and realizes what he's done."

"What do you folks do?"

"Search the boat, call the cops, and the car gets towed away. Gets messy, I'm tellin yah."

Frank realizes he's holding them up and says, "Guess I better get off here."

After calling from Bremerton and getting the instructions, he drove north out of Bremerton toward Brownsville. When he made the turn off, he wound down around until he passed the small auto repair garage, then around the small store-service station combination. He turned right again toward the marina and followed the road up around to the left until he came to the road he was looking for. Then he turned onto the road, and found the house at the end of the small street. As he got out of his car, he walked up the short driveway to the house. Just outside the open garage door he found a short wiry man in his mid sixties working with a metal detector swaying it back and forth over a small bolt on top of a patch of the grass near the garage. "Mr. Andrews?"

"Yep." He said as he looked up at Frank. "You Chambers?"

"Yessir," Frank answered in a polite, but respectful, manner.

"Pull up a seat young fella," Fred Andrews said, indicating a nearby sawhorse. Frank tried to make himself comfortable on its two inch edge.

Mr. Andrews finalized his adjustments on the metal detector and pulled up an empty five gallon can. He turned it upside down and sat on it. "What can I do for yah?"

"Actually, Mr.Andrews, it may be more of what I can do for you."

Frank began asking him several questions in such a manner that would allow him to decide if he needed to consider Mr. Andrews a suspect in this case. His last question had cinched it. He had asked Mr. Andrews, "You read the paper every day by any chance?"

"Naw. Don't even take the damn thing. Just full'a junk these days, a waste of good money and trees to even print it."

Satisfied, Frank began slowly explaining what had been taking place, not in detail, but enough to get the message across. "My concern, Mr. Andrews, is that I'm pretty sure you are, or could be the next person on the list."

"Kinda scary ain't it?"

"Yes, it is. I can try to arrange some kind of protection for you."

"Haft'a be a mighty good country boy, if you did."

"Why's that?"

"Coupla more days an I'll be gone up to my mine, won't be back until my supplies run out."

"Anybody you've played chess with know where your mine is ?"

"I doubt it. Never tell many folks, cause it's my get away."

"If I needed to find you, how'd I go about it?"

Fred Andrews thought about it for a few seconds, then made his decision. He got up off his five gallon can and walked over to his work bench in the garage pulled a sheet of scratch paper off a pad and started to draw a map. When he finished it, he returned to where Frank was still seated, and handed it to Frank.

"Don't you give this to anybody, yah hear?"

Frank grinned as if he'd just been given a treasure map. "No problem."

"Local Forest Ranger knows my place and can find me if need be. You'd just call them, an they'd get a message up to my place."

Frank thanked him, said goodby, and on the way down the driveway he decided he'd call the forest ranger up there and have him keep an eye on Fred Andrews without making it seem apparent that that was what he was doing.

SEARCHING FOR ANDREWS

He had found the phone number and had tried to call just to be sure the man he wanted to see was home. He wasn't having any luck that way as no one answered it. Finally he knew there wasn't any other way, so he drove his old Ford down to the ferry landing at Mukilteo, where he waited two hours for the ferry. It turned out to be an all day trip because of the time and distance involved. The next leg of the trip was catching the ferry across to Port Townsend from Whidbey Island, then he drove down to Brownsville from there.

Once he located the street, he parked at the open end of the cross street, and walked down the street toward the Andrews home as if he were just out for a quiet afternoon stroll. When he got to the end of the street, he stopped to look at the view. An elderly lady was outside tending to one of her shrubs near the cedar rail fence. On his way back toward his car he stopped by her and said, "I haven't seen Fred Andrews around the last coupla days, have you?"

The older woman looked at him quizzically. He wasn't familiar to her, but he knew her neighbor's name, *'Must be new in the area,'* she thought. "I think he's off on another one a his trip's up'ta his gold mine in the mountains."

"Oh. Could be I suppose." He smiled, then turned away and headed for his car.

Well, that would explain no answer on the telephone. "Now what the hell do I do?" He couldn't wait forever, yet Andrews was an unfinished loose end of what he had set out to accomplish.

He hated to take them out of turn, and he had no idea of where Andrews might have gone off to, or how to find out that information without being too conspicuous about it.

BUREAU OF LAND MANAGEMENT

He hadn't wanted to go into Seattle, mostly because of the heavier traffic, but also because he was afraid someone might recognize him while in the city. Yet it seemed the only way to get the information he wanted. He'd finally had to park in a paid parking lot because there weren't any parking spaces on the street opening up, just people coming out of various buildings and feeding their meters. He often wondered which was the cheaper, paying for a parking meter all day or paying to park in a lot where you didn't have to concern yourself whether you were still legal on the meter and worrying about a meter maid coming by to ticket your car.

He walked the three blocks to the old building, went up the granite stairs with the highly polished brass hand rails and inside the building. Once he was inside, he found the building's occupant register, scanned it quickly and saw the department he wanted.

WASHINGTON STATE DEPARTMENT OF THE INTERIOR. When he found it, the door was blocked open. He asked a middle aged woman at the counter where he could get some information about old mines and mining claims.

"Go out this door, turn right and upstairs to the Bureau of Land Management, they probably can help you." He walked up the flight of marble stairs. As he passed a woman coming down, he listened to her high heels clicking loudly on the hard floor. It always surprised him how such small women made so much noise when they walked in high heels, as if they were digging in to get a grip on the floor.

As he walked down the hall, he caught a glimpse of a sign over a doorway that was across the hall from the Bureau of Land Management, which had been his destination. It read,

'MINING CLAIMS AND REGISTRATION. He went into this office instead.

Inside the office he walked to the counter and a young man who didn't look like he was old enough to be working here, was looking through a book of records on the other side. "Can I help you?" He said as he looked up.

"Yeah, listen I've got this old family friend who asked me if I'd like to invest in a gold mine. I didn't want to insult him by asking him if he really owned a gold mine, so I told him I'd think about it for a couple of days and get back to him."

"I see," the young man said, smiling. "Well I could look it up to see if he has a valid mining claim if you like."

"I'd appreciate that. I mean, I like the old guy. Still, I'd like to know if he really has a legitimate mine."

The young man behind the counter hesitated. Then said, "I'm sorry but there's a fee involved."

"No problem." He reached for his wallet.

"What's his name?"

"Andrews, Fred Andrews"

The younger man went to a small metal file box on top

of a larger file cabinet and removed a few sheets of nearly transparent film. He consulted the few slips of microfiche, then after a few minutes he said, "Up in the Okanagon?"

"That'd be the place." He was pleased that this seemed to be working out so well.

"Yeah, looks like it's a valid claim. Hang on a bit I'll get you a plot chart of his holdings." In less than ten minutes he had just what he needed to find Fred Andrews.

Death to The Queen

R			Q	K	B	N	R
P	P	P			P	P	
			P				P
						$\mathcal{B}$	
		N		$\mathcal{P}$			
		$\mathcal{N}$	$\mathcal{P}$				
$\mathcal{P}$	$\mathcal{P}$	$\mathcal{P}$				$\mathcal{P}$	$\mathcal{P}$
$\mathcal{R}$			B	$\mathcal{K}$			$\mathcal{R}$

QBXQ

THIRD MONDAY IN MARCH

Frank had been laying awake for better than an hour. Finally, he'd gotten up out of bed and picked up his pants as he crept out of Cary Ann's bedroom. He stopped outside her bedroom door, pulled his pants on then walked into her kitchen. Cary Ann's kitchen was an exhibition of cleanliness compared to his. Frank even hated making coffee, afraid he might leave a mess of some sort. He finished getting the coffee grounds into the filter, and the water poured into the top of the coffee maker.

Now, satisfied he had everything done correctly, he put the can of coffee away and cleaned up. It seemed like it was only seconds before the coffee started to drip down into the glass pot. He left it to work its magic while he went out onto the front porch for the morning paper. It was trying to rain.

He had two coffee cups on the table, his was full of coffee, hers was empty but waiting for her when she got up. Scanning the newspaper, he saw what he had been dreading. Without trying to be quiet now, he pushed the bedroom door open and finished dressing hurriedly. Cary Ann was half awake when he came in. She propped herself up on an elbow, watching him rushing to get dressed. "What's up?"

"Got'ta get to the office." He finished pulling his shoes and socks on, tucked his shirt into the top of his pants and grabbed his jacket. Before he pulled it on, he leaned over and kissed her. He wanted to get back into bed with her but said, "Sorry, got'ta run. See ya later, okay?" Before she could answer, he was out the door.

"God, you should'a shaved anyway," she was saying to his foot steps as they faded from the front porch. A little later after she had taken her morning shower, dressed and gone to the kitchen, she found the coffee already made. Cary Ann poured herself a cup of coffee and sat down at the table. She looked down to the personals column that Frank had left open and she began to read them.

"Oh, no!" Was all she said as she looked at the ad. It read "QBXQ -------"

OFFICE

It was after ten o'clock in the morning before anyone answered the telephone. Frank had been trying for better than an hour to contact the Forest Ranger Station up in the high country. Dave Fuller had heard the phone ringing when he drove up to the front of the division of forestry building in his four wheel drive government vehicle. He had been in such a hurry to get to the phone, he left his keys hanging in the lock of the front door. Out of breath he answered "Ranger Station," forgetting all normal answering protocol that he normally went through.

"Yes, who's this please?"

"I'm Dave Fuller, the duty ranger at the moment."

"Dave, this is Detective Frank Chambers, I. . . ."
Before Frank could tell Dave Fuller why he was calling, Dave interrupted him.

"Oh, sure, Mr. Chambers. I remember talking with you the other day."

Frank went blank, then he said, "Have we met?"

"Sure. Don't you remember? You called me before, and it was me you talked to the other day when you were up here."

Curious now, Frank said, "What do I look like?"

"Kinda tall, black hair, kinda slim." Dave thought that was a strange question but he had answered it anyway.

"Bald spot on the top of the head?" Frank asked.

"Yeah."

"Dave that wasn't me. I haven't been up there."

"I wonder who it was then. Said he was you."

Without answering, Frank said, "Dave, have you got a sheriff's department anywhere nearby up there?"

"Yeah, sheriffs' name is Bill Williams. He's only about nine miles from here. Want his number?"

"Please." Frank made a note of the telephone number as it was given to him, then continued, "Dave stay at your office for a while, will you. The Sheriff may call you."

"Sure, I can get caught up on some paper work."

Frank pushed the off button on the phone, then after getting dial tone he called the number for the Sheriff's Office. Sheriff Williams was just about to go for coffee when his phone rang. "Sheriff's Office."

"Is this Sheriff Bill Williams?"

"That's right."

"Sheriff, this is Detective Frank Chambers. I'm working on a case and I need your help." Frank went on to finish giving the sheriff some basic background about the case he was working on and his own office phone number, then said, "My concern is for Mr. Fred Andrews. He's got a mine up in your local area

229

somewhere. The Forest Ranger, Dave Fuller is supposed to know where it is. Do you know Mr. Fuller?"

"Oh sure. We work together occasionally around here on different matters."

Frank continued. "The problem is that I can't get up to Mr. Andrew's mine as quick as you fellas can, and I fear for his safety. I'd appreciate it if you'd go up and check on him for me."

"Sure we can do that for ya. When do you need this done?"

"As soon as possible, and Sheriff, one more thing. I'm hoping you'll find Mr. Andrews in good health, but you might want'a be prepared to find a homicide situation."

BURIED ALIVE

It had been much easier than he thought it would be. He'd arrived at the Division of Forestry Ranger Station to ask for further directions. As he walked up the steps to the building, the Ranger came out of the door. Apparently the Ranger was on his way somewhere else. He interrupted the Rangers thoughts when he casually asked for directions up to the Andrews mine. The Ranger looked up and said, "You Chambers." The Ranger hadn't made a direct question, more of a statement. The ranger seemed to think he was someone else. Then, before he could even answer the man in uniform, and without hesitation, he just gave him the directions to the mine.

He had driven his old Ford slowly up the wet and rutted road for what seemed like hours, but wasn't. He could see the mine tailings on the side of the mountain in the distance so he stopped well short of the mine and pulled his car off the road into a small stand of trees. The ground was firm under the trees with small branches and pine needles blanketing all the open ground available. Then he walked the rest of the way into his destination.

When he arrived near the mine he watched for awhile from a safe distance where he was hidden in the brush and, finally, he was rewarded with the man's appearance. Andrews came out of the small cabin on a rise by itself and slowly walked up to the mine entrance. He loaded an arm full of equipment into a small ore rail car, and began pushing the ore car slowly on the steel rails into the mine shaft.

When he thought it was safe to move again, without being seen, he crept up to the mine shaft. Carefully leaning around a large support pillar, he peeked inside. Just a short distance inside the rocky opening he saw some cases marked BLASTING POWDER.

He could also hear some noise deeper inside the mine's interior. Quickly and quietly he worked his way inside walking on the small railroad ties to keep the noise of his foot steps to a minimum, listening as he went. As he came closer to one of the turns in the tunnel, he could hear the noise more clearly. It was the sound of metal striking metal, a small sledge striking an iron star drill. As he started back out of the tunnel, he noticed one of the support beams holding several big pieces of heavy support timbers in place over head.

Back at the mine's entrance he picked up a case of blasting powder and a long fuse. Returning, he placed the nearly full case of dynamite near the base of the main support beam, and pulled one stick of dynamite out. With his pocket knife opened he pushed a hole into the end of the stick of dynamite with the small knife blade, then pushed the blasting cap down into the opening he'd made. He placed this stick of dynamite in with the others in the case at his feet.

Fred had been so busy handling the drill steel that he'd worked up a thirst. Deciding to cure it, he started toward the mine entrance. On the way out of the tunnel he was thinking that if he'd only remembered to pick up his canteen and bring it in with him, he wouldn't be making this trip out right now. When he rounded the last turn where he could see some distance ahead of him, he saw the man looking back at him.

A split second after their eyes met, the man disappeared out of sight around the edge of the mine entrance. Fred also saw the smoke from the burning fuse working its way rapidly toward the case of dynamite. He knew he could not get past the danger in time, so he turned around to run. Just after he got turned, and had run a short distance, he felt the harsh blast lift him up and throw him forward along side the tracks. Critically injured and just before he died, he picked up a rock with his hand and in the dark pushed it against the hard rock wall near his out stretched arm.

MINE

Sheriff Bill Williams was waiting in his pickup truck for the forest ranger, Dave Fuller, to finish locking up his office. Finished, Dave opened the truck's door and stepped up onto the high running board to get into the truck's cab. In and settled with his seat belt in place, the sheriff backed the truck up and headed south east.

"You're gonna tell me where we're going, right?"

"Umm . . . Yeah." Dave said as he was still getting himself comfortable. " Straight ahead. It's the third road on the left after you go around the long left turn in the highway."

They drove in silence for about fifteen minutes when Dave said, "There, just ahead. See it, Bill?"

"Yeah." He started to slow down to make the turn off. They waited for two cars to go by in the opposite lane, then Bill turned his pickup left and onto a gravel road. They had only driven a few hundred feet when the gravel began to run out leaving mostly dirt and rough rocks. "This a county road or Division of Forestry?"

"Division of Forestry, and it sure needs some work."

"You got that right. Glad I brought the pickup instead of my patrol car."

"They won't do much about it this year. I think they plan to take a road grader to it next year and maybe add some more gravel."

234

They drove along the rough road dodging the deeper ruts as they went. As they neared the mine road Dave was looking for, he pointed it out to the sheriff. "Turn right just up ahead."

Just as they turned, Bill pulled at the steering wheel trying to miss one large rock in the road. Doing so he missed seeing the tire tracks leading off to the right and up into a small clearing under some nearby pine trees. After they left the forestry road, the road to the mine and its buildings was in much better condition.

Bill parked the pickup just below the small cabin. They got out and walked up to the cabin where Dave knocked on the door. Not receiving an answer, Dave walked to a window and looked in. He saw nothing and said so to Bill. Bill tried the door knob and the door opened. They walked inside calling out. "Mr. Andrews it's Sheriff Bill Williams." A few seconds passed and "Mr. Andrews?" Satisfied after they finished looking around that he wasn't in the cabin, they walked back out onto the porch of the cabin, pulled the door closed behind them and began to look around outside.

"Oh oh!" Bill said.

"What."

"Look up there at the mine. Look odd to you?"

"Damn. Looks like there's a lotta rocks at the entrance. We better have a look."

They walked down the slight incline from the cabin then up another incline to the mine's entrance. When they arrived, they both searched around the rock filled entrance calling out to Fred Andrews as they moved around the pile of rocks that blocked any effort to get inside the mine.

Dave finally moved back away from the entrance saying, "Looks pretty hopeless doesn't it?"

"Fraid so. We might as well go back to town. I'll see if I can round up some help to come back up here and dig this out. Andrews might be inside."

"I might be able to get some of our fella's to come along too."

Early the next day the weather turned out decent as some of the county work crew, forestry men, and a couple of off duty deputies rode up in a county transport van.

The back of the sheriff's pickup truck was full of tools they thought they might need. They worked hard nearly all day moving rocks and debris away from the mine entrance. As they worked their way in, they were careful not to disturb anything that looked as though it might bring more rocks down into the mine tunnel. Late in the day a hole large enough to crawl through on ones hands and knee's was opened. The Sheriff and one of his deputies crawled inside slowly, and very carefully. Inside the tunnel, the air was musty and damp. They picked their way slowly up the tunnel following the tracks as they went. Just as they came to a turn, the beam of the Sheriff's flashlight flashed across something. Bill said, "Watch out. He's right there in front of us."

When they reached the body Bill played his flashlight around the area looking the situation over carefully. "Strange." He said as he knelt down next to the body.

The deputy asked, "What's strange?"

Bill looked up from his position next to the dead man. "He's got a sharp rock in his hand."

SHERIFF'S CALL

Jim answered the phone when it rang, giving his name as he did so. He listened for a few seconds then said, "Yes he's here, hang on." He got up out of his chair and walked down the hall to where Sergeant Brown was talking with Frank. "Frank. It's that sheriff you've been waiting to hear from."

"See ya, Mike," Frank said as he turned, heading back for his office. After he settled into his chair, he picked up the telephone saying, "Frank Chambers here."

"Detective, I'm sorry to have to tell you this but, it seems Mr. Andrews was killed in an explosion at his mine."

Frank was dismayed. He'd thought the old guy would be safe up there. "Did he die from the explosion itself or by some other means?"

"Couldn't tell you that yet, have'ta finish digging him out first."

"How long will that take?"

"Coupla day's, I 'spect. I'll let you know when we can get inside safely."

"Thanks Sheriff." Frank hung up the phone, turned to Jim and said, "Dammit Jim, Fred Andrews has been killed." Now he knew there were only two chess players left. He had to do something, but what?

OFFICE, TWO DAYS LATER

Frank had called Jennie at the newspaper office and asked her to place another ad for him in the personal column. She agreed to do that for him and verified again, "I want to be sure I do this right. If someone calls about this chess move or the game, I can give your home phone number out, but to use the name of Ted Brewster as the person who placed the ad."

"Yes, that's the way I'd like it done," Frank agreed.

Just after nine A.M. the phone rang and he picked it up. "Detective Chambers," he answered.

"Mr. Chambers, this is Dave Fuller, I'm calling for Sheriff Williams. He's up at Mr. Andrews cabin keeping a watch over the place. He thinks you might wanna come up here. He's got somethin' he thinks you might be interested in."

Without hesitation, Frank said, "Sure, be a few hours though before I can get there."

"No problem. When you get here, come to my office first, and I'll take you up."

It was after lunch before Frank arrived at the Ranger Station. He walked into the office and introduced himself to Dave Fuller. They talked briefly as Dave picked his jacket up off a chair next to his desk and they went out to Dave's four wheel drive jeep, locking the door behind them. On the trip up the mountain road, Frank had asked Dave if he could remember anything else about the man who had asked directions to the Andrews mine property.

"No, not much more than what I've told you."

Dave had explained how he'd thought it was Frank just coming by his office to check on Mr. Andrews. Both men knew this mistake had possibly cost Mr. Andrews his life.

"Did you see the car this guy was driving?"

"UMmm. Yeah. Seems like it was one of those old Ford Mavericks. A blue one, the paint was kinda washed out from lack of care."

"I don't suppose you got a license number by any chance?"

"Never thought about doing that, but I did see it. I remember it was one of those kinda license plates you don't see too often."

"You mean a special personal plate?"

"I don't recall if it was one of those custom plates or not but it was different somehow. Seems like everything was in a straight sequence of some kind."

"Straight sequence?"

"Yeah, you know, like one, two, three, or somethin."

"Year?"

"You mean the car?"

"Yeah."

"Dunno, maybe early seventies?"

As they drove the last of the distance up to the mine, the Sheriff had seen them coming from the Andrews cabin and walked down to his car that was parked just a short distance down the hill from the cabin, to meet them. As Frank climbed down from the high seat of the jeep, he took the Sheriff's hand introducing himself.

They started walking up the incline toward the mine opening. Up at the mine they talked about the rocks that now lay in a huge pile outside the mine entrance. The Sheriff explained how he'd gotten some local folks to help dig it out of the mine and how they'd had to shore up part of the mine's entrance as they went in. The Sheriff explained that Mr. Andrews had been killed by the blast and flying debris. They walked slowly into the mine, all three of them carrying large flash lights as they went. Just at the turn in the tunnel, the Sheriff stopped, and indicated with his finger, "That's where we found him, right there."

They moved over to the spot, then the Sheriff bent down. Frank, following his lead, did the same and looked to where Bill's finger was pointing. They were looking at some marks on the nearby rock wall. Frank got down on his hands and knees and looked closer. What he saw was something scratched into the rock.

"Looks like letters. What's it say?"

"That's what puzzles me." The Sheriff said. "Best I can make out he was trying to tell us something."

"Looks like an E..V..E...N...Z."

"Yeah, of course in the dark he couldn't see what he was writing, or where, but that's about what I made it out to be. I agree with you."

Death to The Queen's

R			*B*	K	B	N	R
P	P	P			P	P	
			P				P
		N		*P*			
		N	*P*				
P	*P*	*P*				*P*	*P*
R			B	*K*			*R*

BXQ

INVITATION

He'd stopped to pick up the newspaper while he was in the small downtown area of the island, but didn't stop to read it while he was there. Instead he'd waited until he was back at the cabin and he hadn't wasted any time in his driving to get back to the cabin. Inside he stoked the fire in the stove back to life bringing some warmth with it. He added two more pieces of fire wood, then went to the small table near the window that overlooked a small portion of the bay nearby. He began to read the paper slowly, finally getting to the personal ad section. He'd read it but wasn't sure what it said. Had he read it correctly? He looked again. It hadn't changed.

9. QBXQ ------ BXQ,---Want to play a game?

At first he seemed confused searching for an answer. Then, after he thought about it awhile, he pondered the possible potential and repercussions. He found the thought rather intriguing. This person couldn't know who he was. *'What could be the harm in it?'* Then he voiced it out loud. "Couldn't hurt."

DMV RECORDS

Frank finally got the computer printout from the Department of Motor vehicles. He had asked for all the files of license plate numbers of 1973 to 1976 Ford Mavericks starting with any sequence of license numbers in a row, such as 1-2-3. It was huge. Its twenty seven and a third printed pages consisted of one thousand and ninety two listings.

He had started by going through the list looking for a hint to the original factory colors then decided that wasn't the way to go about it. So he started looking for some kind of sequential numbering that looked like what he wanted instead. Out of the original list, when he had finished, there were only sixty three entries that started with the numbers 1-2-3 plus various letters following. There were a few that started with 2-3-4, a few with 3-4-5 and a few with 4-5-6.

It had taken Frank all morning, and most of the early afternoon to go through the list. He'd started using different colored marking pens for the different number sequences but gave that endeavor up after awhile. He was envisioning checking out all the cars himself, a job he knew would be monumental. He thought maybe he could use Kim Larson and Don Olson, the two detectives who were working the evening shift. Kim and Don often had some slack periods of time in the evenings while they were making their normal rounds. He also knew they had a king sized drug case they were working on and he hated to ask but he would. He'd ask Jim as well. He knew it would take him much too long to do it all himself and it was too large to give to the patrol cars on the street.

Frank typed up a separate list of the sixty three cars with sequential license plate numbers then made copies of the list for the others as well. He had been studying the list again without really thinking, his mind almost a blank because of the amount of time he had spent on the list to this point. He was about to call it a day and it was just a few minutes after four in the afternoon, when he checked the list one last time. Running his finger down the list, he stopped and, his eyes scanning back up the list, he moved his finger back up to one of the cars listed. Its license number just struck him, 123-ABC.

"How come I didn't notice this one before?" He thought. Quickly he dialed the phone number of the Forestry Station and Dave Fuller's office. He was just about to give up on the call when Dave answered the phone. "Ranger Station."

"Dave?"

"Yes. Who's this?"

"Dave, this is Frank Chambers."

"Oh sure. How'ya doin, Frank?"

"Fine, Dave. Say listen, didn't you tell me that the car that the guy was driving, you know the one we discussed had a license plate number that was in line, or sequential I think you said?"

"If I remember correctly, yes."

"Does 123-ABC sound familiar to you?"

"That's it, at least I think that's it."

The next day Frank had driven out to the Ford,s registered owner's home. It didn't surprise Frank. He encountered the same condition of ownership that he and Jim had found with the Volvo owner. The owner of the Ford had sold it earlier, and couldn't help Frank as to its present location or anything about the new owner.

Frank had given him a description of the same person who had purchased the Volvo but the man who had owned the Ford didn't remember much about the man. It had been late at night when he'd come for the car and it had been dark. The car was out there somewhere, but where, and who had it?
Before Frank left the office, he'd decided to put this one license number out on the statewide system. Every patrol car in the state would have the license number and would be watching for it.

CHIEF'S CONFERENCE

When Frank first arrived in his office, he'd removed his files from his desk drawer and gone carefully through his notes. He looked slowly through them again. His mind was making mental notes as he read through them for the umpteenth time., He wanted to be ready with answers for any questions the Chief might have about this case or Frank's feeling about it. When he was ready, he went down the hall and walked into the Chief's office at five minutes past eight.

Once inside the chief's office, the chief greeted him with, "Good morning Frank. Come in, come in, make yourself comfortable, I'll be right with you."

Frank sat in a large plush chair, the one farthest from the door but the nearest one to the chief's desk. *'This was probably the only office in the building that had chairs as nice to sit in as these were.'* He thought to himself.

Chief Peters finished reading one of his many reports, then he put it on top of a stack of files that teetered on the edge of the desk. It looked as though the whole stack might just slide off onto the floor at any moment.

"Well, Frank, how's your theory about this chess killer working out?" The chief was well aware of the idea Frank was pursuing now. He'd known for several reasons. The short discussion with Frank before, Frank's monthly reports, the time card entries he and Jim were making, plus the phone call he'd received from the police chief on Whidbey Island, and he'd heard others around the office talking about it as well. It wasn't as if he were the last to know about it.

248

"I'm making progress, but it's slow." Frank was well aware he had used a great deal of time on this case and so far it was mostly circumstantial. There was really nothing concrete to go on, mostly his own feelings, but there was a pattern that he could show to anyone now. He didn't mention the latest report he had received from Sheriff Williams. The report from Sheriff Williams was filed with the rest of the information he had on his lap in front of him.

- -

ACCIDENTAL DEATH REPORT FORM.
Fred Andrews
Killed in an explosion in mine shaft.
Time of death - approximate 04:15 P.M.
Circumstances - Appeared he had stored dynamite in the mine shaft and an accidental explosion took place.

Note:
Curiously the investigation revealed a few letters were scratched into the surface of a nearby rock.
Sheriff Williams considers this death a possible homicide.
The letters scratched into the rocks appeared
to be E-V-E-N-Z.

- -

After he'd given some basic information to the chief about the daily affairs of the detective squad, the chief asked him, "Frank why are you pursuing this case so hard?"

Frank had to search his feelings for a few moments, but satisfied with what he felt, he said, "I think it's because these are homicides and this killer might have gotten away with the deaths entirely if I hadn't been curious enough, and began to look into a few things about each individual involved."

"You don't have any personal connection with any of these people?"

"No sir. I just found it a challenge to get to the bottom of what are some very strange coincidences."

"Okay Frank. Why don't you give me a detailed update on this thing."

Frank took his time making his report to the chief about the chess killer case. He knew he needed to present a good strong case to justify spending more departmental time on it. He presented all of his facts about the case hoping he'd done a good job of it. How it had started out and how it had developed over a period of time. When he was done, he said, "And that's why I'm sure this is a methodical serial killer going through a preselected list of people."

The chief was well aware of the time spent so far and knew Frank was a competent detective. The chief had decided before Frank had even come into his office, to allow him the time he needed. Accidental deaths were one thing. Murder was something else again. "Need any help?"

"No, Sir. Jim helps me on occasion when I need it. Trouble is this guy had killed several people before I stumbled onto him."

"And he might'a gotten away with it, if you hadn't been curious." The Chief was pleased with the fact that it had been one of his officers who had stumbled across this case. Otherwise, the deaths might have been passed off as accidental. Plus it was something he could tell the police commissioner about over lunch or dinner. In a sense this was an unusual case that one of his men had discovered and it would show the efficiency of how well his department was running, a feather in his own cap as well as Frank's.

"Yeah, he might have."

"You've still got leads to follow up on. You have a direction to follow?"

"Yessir, several."

"Okay, Frank. I'm gonna go along with you on this, but I need more hard evidence on this thing to present to a district attorney. So far it's rather sketchy."

"Yessir, I'll do what I can."

"Anything else I can do, let me know, okay?"

Frank hesitated briefly then he took a chance and said, "There is one other thing I could use."

"Which is?"

"Some court orders to check into the victims personal records such as bank accounts, and so on."

"Humm that could be tough to arrange." Frank could see the chief was scanning his sources mentally.

Finally he went on to say, "Let me talk to the man to see what I can arrange."

"Yes sir, and thanks."

On the way back to his office he was thinking about the fact that there were only two men left on the list that he knew about at the time. Also he wondered who the man was the chief had made reference too. Probably Judge Herman.

After Frank left the office he was elated. He was sure he had sold the chief on the case and could now devote much more of his time to it. Frank spent, over an hour driving in the ongoing crowded morning traffic north on Highway five until he turned off at the off ramp, driven down to the docks and reached the charter office. He had called the charter office earlier and arranged with Mr. Jenkins, the Manager. Frank wanted to interview the crew of the "Largo."

Mr. Jenkins had arranged for Frank to use the small conference room that they used when he and Jim were here the first time. The crew of nine people had been expecting him and seemed relaxed as they came in. Each felt at ease as they spoke with him. None of them seemed nervous, and none could recall anyone causing any problems while onboard the Largo. They couldn't recall anyone being upset with anyone else during the trip, or while they were in Canada. Frank came away from the interviews with the feeling that these folks were so used to catering to a customer's needs, that they somewhat blended in together. Their world was just to serve the needs of others, and not to be too discriminating in their judgements of others.

That afternoon when Frank was back in Seattle, he made a side trip down to the lake area and spoke with the flight dock attendant who had been on duty the day Jacques Quine had flown out from the lake. The flight dock attendant had been very cooperative but of little use to Frank. The dock attendant was just used to seeing so many people come and go, that no one had stood out any differently than anyone else.

When he was finally back at the office, he and Jim were going over the case when Frank said, "One thing that puzzles me is, why this guy Andrews would scratch the letter's EVENZ, OR EVENS on the rocks where he died. It doesn't make any sense."

"Unless he didn't, or couldn't finish scratching out his message." Jim said.

"What else could he have added to EVEN with a Z?"

"Beats me. Even saying EVEN STEVEN, you know that old saying, wouldn't really mean too much because you wouldn't know who he was talking about."

"Has to be something though. Something important, especially when he had to scratch it into a rock, in the dark, while he was dying."

Your move - Game two

R	N	B	Q	K	B	N	R
P	P	P	P	P	P	P	P
			$\mathcal{P}$				
$\mathcal{P}$	$\mathcal{P}$	$\mathcal{P}$	$\mathcal{P}$		$\mathcal{P}$	$\mathcal{P}$	$\mathcal{P}$
$\mathcal{R}$	$\mathcal{N}$	$\mathcal{B}$	$\mathcal{Q}$	$\mathcal{K}$	$\mathcal{B}$	$\mathcal{N}$	$\mathcal{R}$

P-K4

GAME OFFER

Two weeks passed since Frank had placed the advertisement in the paper as to the ninth move in the chess game. This same advertisement had carried an offer to play a game of chess across the board. Now Frank was reading the personals column while he sat eating breakfast. The first thing that caught his eye was the listing saying Game #2 1. P-k4 --------.

"Whoa, game two?" Frank thought. I don't understand this, is he offering me a game, or is this the beginning of a new killing spree? Frank didn't bother finishing his breakfast and left it all sitting on his kitchen table. He rushed about getting his stuff together, and hurried to work. He drove faster to work than he would normally. Once Frank arrived at the office, he had gone to the coffee shop for coffee in the largest container he could find. A few minutes later he was in Cary Ann's office, pacing. All other things had seemed to come to a stop while he waited for the morning reports to come in. When Cary Ann handed them to him, he reached out quickly, pulled them from her fingers and headed toward his office. He walked a few steps then turned.

"Sorry, Cary. Thanks for the report."

She knew he was concerned, and she knew that something different must have happened. She also knew she would have to ask him about it later because his mind was in high gear somewhere else besides here with her.

He'd gone to his office where he read the computer report again while he sat at his desk. Nothing! He thanked God that nothing had happened that seemed to fit the pattern of accidents he was used to seeing.

255

Finally he happened to think of what might be happening with the game in the newspaper, so he called Jennie at the newspaper and had her place his ad in the paper.

"Game 2 P-K4 -- Not here, takes too much time. How about a game across the board?"

He knew that he had to make some kind of attempt to draw this player out into the open. He also knew he couldn't play chess well enough to play a proper game against his suspected killer. He decided that he would talk to Ted and ask him to be the opposing player in the game if the chess killer agreed to play a chess game openly.

ELDRIDGE

Frank rang the doorbell, waited a few minutes, then rang it again. Shortly the door opened slowly to reveal a man in his sixties, but who looked as though he was ten years younger than his age. His hair was still dark with color, and his skin relatively free of wrinkles and he had a general youthful look about him.

"Mr. Eldridge, I'm Frank Chambers, I called you earlier."

"Oh sure, come in, come in. We've been expecting you."

Frank followed him as they walked through a large open and muggy foyer. It felt like a small botanical garden. A fountain just off center in the room gave off a comforting gurgling sound of splashing water. Greenery of various types crowded the area as well. Frank wondered how much dry rot the wooden framing of this part of the house was suffering from with this much constant humidity.

Then they walked through two large sliding glass doors and through a large living area that looked out onto Puget Sound. The windows in this room ran from wall to wall, which appeared to be a distance of about thirty feet across. A huge fireplace built into the southern wall didn't look like it had ever had a fire burning in its interior. Harvey Eldridge turned back toward him and motioned Frank through another door leading outside. "I was out here when you rang the door bell," he said.

When Frank exited the main house, he saw a woman who was apparently a few years younger than Harvey. She was sitting at a large white ornate patio deck table. She turned to face them as they approached. Harvey said "Mr. Chambers, this is my lady and wife of some thirty years, Marcy. Frank sank into a very comfortable chair he'd been offered at the table.

"Please call me Frank." He said. "Marcy, I'm glad to meet you."

She smiled, her wide mouth saying, "Frank, can I get you a lemonade?"

"Why, yes, please. I'd like that." Frank could tell Marcy had been used to entertaining guests in her home. He could hear the sound of the old south in her voice, like southern ladies of the past. Frank figured this probably came from the area where she had been raised as a child. If this were the case, entertaining in the home would be second nature to her.

Harvey Eldridge said, "Frank if you're chilly we could go inside the house. Marcy and I were out here to watch the sunset."

The patio they were sitting on at the back of the house, was enclosed just enough on three sides to keep most of the weather from effecting it. "Actually, it's quite nice out and I welcome the chance to share it with you."

Frank didn't often get to enjoy this kind of intimate time with others in his line of work. Even now he hated to spoil it with business.

Frank slowly sipped the lemonade Marcy had gotten him, enjoying its tart flavor. The pleasure of homemade lemonade was something he hadn't had in years. The deck at the back of the house was large with an excellent view up the sound. Just below them on the open waters of a small protected cove Frank could see a sail boat dropping an anchor into the dark green water. He watched as the man at the bow of the boat lowered the anchor into the water, while using hand signals to his mate at the helm. It seemed like it was only seconds before they were finished getting the anchor set into the bottom silt and sand before a boom tent went up in place over the boat's main sail boom shading the boat's cockpit. The fact that they worked as a team was very apparent.

His thoughts of where he was, and why he was here had escaped him briefly. Then he heard, "Mr. Chambers. . . . I mean Frank, I realize you didn't come for a social visit, so how can I help you?"

Frank was hesitant. He didn't want to spoil the quiet and comfortable evening they had been enjoying thus far, but he knew he had to. "Mr. Eldridge I'm afraid I have some news that is, ummm, frankly a little scary. However, you must be aware of all of the circumstances involved."

Frank had already determined that these folks were not implicated in the deaths of the others in any way. Slowly he continued to explain how things had happened in each of the deaths of the other chess players. When he had finished, Harvey, who had paid strict attention to what Frank had told them, said, "You mean Andy Tatum and I are the only ones left alive?"

"Of the final tournament players, yes. To the best of my knowledge everyone else that was on the boat is still alive and well."

"Is what you're saying to me, that you think I'm going to be killed?" He and Marcy were wide eyed considering the possibilities.

"I cannot at this time say you're not in danger, because I think you are. Because of that, and with your permission, I'd like to have a team of men watching you and your house full time."

Harvey looked at Marcy, saying, "Is that okay with you sweetie?"

"Of course, sweetheart!" She thought for a moment, then added "We have plenty of room, we could let them stay in the house if you like, Frank."

Frank smiled. The fella's would like that type of stake out. "No, I don't think that'll be necessary, and that might actually hinder their abilities. I would however, like for you two to stay in touch with them, letting them know your intentions ahead of time, at least until I have the situation resolved."

"Frank with you going to all this trouble for us, the least we can do is work with you folks."

There had been a question at the back of Frank's mind that he had intended asking Andrew Tatum but he had almost forgotten what it was. Now he asked, "Harvey, had all of the players in the tournament game played together on more than one occasion?"

"Ummm. . . .yes. Most of us have played chess several times over the years, with the exception of Richard Evans. He was just introduced as a new player."

"How is it Richard Evans came to be in the game?"

"He was a new player, potentially a long term member of the group. He was introduced by Marty Hanson. Seems they were involved together in some real estate projects at one time or another. Also, he had the money to ante up for the game. That is if he made it to the finals, which he did."

Frank had asked this same question of everyone he had interviewed, but he asked it again. "Do you have any thoughts as to who might be involved in this senseless killing and why it would even be taking place?"

"None at all."

"No one stands out in your mind? Anyone who might have been angry, or seemed to be overly upset, any fights or ill feeling caused by something or someone?"

"Not that I can recall. Well, except for Richard of course."

"Richard?"

"Yes, Richard Evans."

"Why him?"

"Well he lost the chance of winning a million dollars, of course."

"Ah. . . . I see. You mean, of course, he lost the last chess game for the prize money?"

"Sure."

"Was he angry?"

"Oh, I doubt it. At least he didn't appear to be but he was under a lot of pressure."

"You were under the same pressure weren't you?"

"Oh, yes. Of course. Well, perhaps, not quite as badly, but I didn't openly sweat over it like Richard did. I can remember seeing the sweat on the top of his head as he played the final match."

"Sweat on the top of his head!" Frank sat up straighter, his curiosity peaked. Wondering how you could see a man with a full head of hair sweat anywhere but on the forehead?

"Sure. As we played, he would lean hunched over the chess board to make his next move each time. When he did, I could see the sweat on the bald spot on the top of his head."

"You mean the spot near the back of his head?" He knew it was a long shot but he asked it.

"That's the place."

Frank had been surprised. He didn't have actual physical descriptions of the players. Frank spent another hour with Harvey and Marcy, then thanked Marcy for the lemonade and found his way out. As he drove back, he was thinking, "My God, this was a direction he hadn't considered. But Evans was dead. Or. . . . was he?"

DMV PHOTOGRAPH

Because of the latest information Frank had stumbled on about the description of Richard Evans, Jim was now involved in trying to get the physical descriptions on all the men who had played in the chess match, also all the crew members of the boat "LARGO". Although most of the tournament chess players that were involved were all dead, or believed to be, it was something that Frank had asked Jim to do.

Frank, himself, had driven down to the Department of Motor Vehicles where he had obtained a photograph of Richard Evans from their files. The photo didn't show anything but a frontal view but it would serve his purposes, then Armed with this and his new information he started making the rounds.

He was driving through the tight, slow, morning commuter traffic, wishing he didn't have to be here. Still, he made good time when he was outside the metropolitan area. It was just after ten o'clock in the morning when he arrived at Dave Fuller's office. He'd called Dave before he'd left town so as not to miss catching him. When he arrived, he parked the unmarked police car in the brown graveled area in front of the forestry building and locked the doors out of habit. The steps up to the porch were of rough rock with a fine cement grout between them, which he thought natural for a Ranger Station. As he pushed the front door open to the division of forestry building, Dave was sitting at a metal desk that looked as though it must have been a military issue at one time.

"Morning, Dave."

"Morning. You want some coffee?"

"Tea, if you've got it."

"Like I said, coffee?" Dave smiled, saying, "You city fella's"

"Coffee." Frank agreed, then after he'd had a sip, he continued, "Any thing new up here?" Not expecting there to be any new developments, just asking as general conversation more than anything else.

"Nope, you?"

Frank reached into his jacket pocket, pulling out the photograph of Richard Evans. He handed it across saying, "Look familiar?"

Dave reached out and nonchalantly took the picture, studied it a few moments, then said,. "So now you know who he is, huh?" Handing the photo back to Frank.

"You've seen him before then?"

"Sure, that's the dude who came looking for Mr. Andrews, and who I thought was you at first."

"That's just what I needed to know, thanks."

Frank and Dave discussed the case in more detail, then Frank had thanked Dave for his help and left Dave's office. He didn't feel any need to stop at the sheriff's office.

On his drive back into the city he headed for Lake Union. He crossed the bridge and turned right down the steep hill. Once at the bottom he turned left to follow the twisted road around the multitude of small businesses and marinas along the shore line. When he arrived at his destination, he had gotten very lucky and found a parking spot near the end of the walk down to the commercial flight dock. The dock attendant was fueling a float plane so he waited and watched with curiosity. As he waited, his eye's traced the fuel lines from the end of the walkway where they came out of the asphalt on the waterfront, then down the ramp and fastened to the side of the floating dock, down to the fuel pumps. The fuel pumps themselves were mounted in the center part of the dock with long fuel hoses that could reach either end of the dock easily. When the attendant had finished fueling the waiting plane and had gotten the credit card slip signed, Frank approached him.

"Hello again."

"You're that detective fella, arn't cha?"

"That's correct. Good memory."

"Well, sometimes."

Frank produced the photo he was using from his jacket pocket, held it out and asked, "Would this by any chance be the mechanic who looked at Jacques Quine's plane before he flew out of here?"

The dock attendant studied the picture for a few moments then offered, "Think so."

"You're sure?"

"Nope, just think so."

266

From here Frank had driven to Andrew Tatum's, then to Harvey Eldridge's, both men acknowledging that the photo was of Richard Evans as they knew him. By now most of the day had passed and he was making his way down the street to Ralph Sawyer's home, when just ahead of him he saw Ralph pulling into his driveway. Frank pulled to the curb just as Ralph got out of his car. He saw Frank and immediately walked over to Frank,s car.

"Evening, Mr. Sawyer."

"How ya doin?"

"Like you to take a look at a photo for me if you will," he said as he opened his car door and climbed out. Then he handed the picture across to Ralph.

"This look like the guy you sold your Volvo to?"

"That's him."

Frank had been very satisfied with his luck during the day as to the identification of Richard Evans as being the person who was now his number one suspect in the case. *'Hah, not my number one suspect, but my only one at this point,'* he was thinking. Back in the police parking lot he had just parked the unmarked car and was walking toward the elevator when the elevator doors opened and Jim walked out. Jim saw him coming and leaned against the fender of his car, waiting. As Frank approached, Jim said, "I've got the descriptions on the men you asked for on your list. It's on your desk."

"May not be necessary now," Frank said as he leaned against Jim's car along side of Jim.

"How's that?"

Frank gave him a run down on the day's events, then followed it with, "I now believe the letters that Mr. Andrews tried to scratch into the rock before he died, were not, "E-V-E-N-Z." But then he said, "I believe it was E-V-A-N-S."

"So you're saying you believe that Richard Evans didn't die from drowning after falling overboard off the ferry?"

"That's my theory. I think he conveniently disappeared."

JIM'S REPORT ON EVANS

The following day, just a few minutes before lunch, Frank returned to the office. Jim had already gone out for lunch but had left a report for him. Frank walked around his desk and, without sitting, he reached down and picked up the sheet of paper, glanced at it, then pulled his chair around and sat down. His feet went up onto the top of his desk, he leaned back in his chair and began to read.

- -

RICHARD EVANS REPORT.
FRANK
I WAS ABLE TO GATHER SOME INFORMATION I BELIEVE WOULD BE CONSISTENT WITH YOUR RECENT FINDING ABOUT MR. EVANS. USING THE INFORMATION YOU GOT FROM THE DEPARTMENT OF MOTOR VEHICLES, I WENT TO THE ADDRESS. UPON ARRIVAL AT THE ADDRESS WE HAD, I FOUND THE CONDO HAD BEEN SOLD, WITH NO FORWARDING ADDRESS.

THE NEIGHBOR ACROSS THE HALL WAS ABLE TO SUPPLY ME WITH THE NAME OF HIS BANK. SHE KNEW IT BECAUSE THEY BOTH USED THE SAME BRANCH. AFTER SPEAKING WITH THE BANK MANAGER, I FOUND HIS ACCOUNT WAS STILL INTACT, BUT HAS NOT BEEN ACTIVE RECENTLY. HOWEVER, HIS LAST WITHDRAWAL WAS SUBSTANTIAL. HE WITHDREW ABOUT TWO HUNDRED AND SEVENTY FIVE THOUSAND DOLLARS IN CASH.

- -

269

Frank was positive now that more and more items were pointing in the direction of Richard Evans as a prime suspect. There was a personal note from Jim attached to the report as well.

Frank

Sorry I missed you this morning. I knew I would need something to convince the bank to give me the information I needed. So I went in to see the chief about a need for one of the court orders you arranged with him. While I was there, he gave me a priority case to work on. I need to devote some time to it, now. It involves an auto accident rip off scam that's going on around the area. See you later.

FRIDAY HARBOR

He'd been in line early this morning so he could catch the first ferry to San Juan Island where he intended to make the phone call to the newspaper. Then after he made the call he would catch the afternoon ferry to Lopez Island and the safety of the cabin on the bay.

When he drove his car down the ramp and onto the ferry, he was the fourth car back in the first center line. He watched the cars behind him fill in the rest of the line he was in, then the next line started along side of him. He climbed out of his Ford with the intention of going up to the snack bar, which doubled for a restaurant.

He was going for some breakfast. When he had walked forward to the metal stairs going to the upper deck area, he happened to look back and saw a police car stop one car behind him in the line next to the one his car was in. His heart rate quickly picked up its pace, even though he realized it was just the Island police on their way back from the mainland.

He ordered his breakfast all the while his eyes searching for any sign of the police approaching. He'd ordered pancakes, but what he ended up with after adding his warm watery syrup, was a soggy mess. His stomach was in a turmoil, but he knew he needed to get some food into it, so he ate this disgusting meal in front of him. He waited, slowly sipping his coffee, but the police officer did not appear. After he left the snack bar, he walked slowly forward, then down to the car deck. When he got to the bottom of the stairs, he walked forward to the front end of the ferry's deck.

Once he was standing near the safety chain, he looked around as if he were just a tourist. What he saw were two police officers looking his car over. After a few moments one of them opened the door to the police car, picked up the mike, keyed it and spoke for a few moments. Then the police officer was apparently waiting for an answer. He knew that for some reason they were investigating the car he had been using. His fear told him the automobile was no longer his to use, and he had to abandon it right where it was.

Just before the ferry reached the island, the speaker system sputtered then a shrill whine emitted from the speakers. Finally a voice asked for the driver of the Blue Ford, license number 123-ABC to report to the car. He had no intention of returning to the car now, he was in line with the walking traffic.

After leaving the warmth of the upper ferry deck, he walked quickly with the other foot traffic up the ramp, past the ticket office. While he mingled in with several other people in a walking group, he glanced down at the cars starting to drive off the ferry. He could not see the police officers but knew they were nearby the car he'd driven onto the ferry. When vehicle traffic leaving the ferry allowed, he walked across the cement automobile loading ramp and boarded an inter island bus marked ROCHE HARBOR. He'd paid the fare, then moved near the rear door of the small bus sitting where he could see most of the ferry landing area. He watched as one of the officers walked up to the walk on passenger ticket area. The police officer was looking around in despair, hoping the person they were seeking was still on board the ferry but also fearing their quarry had gotten away.

On the bus as it drove slowly around the island on its way to Roche Harbor, his mind was racing as he was thinking and searching for answers. 'What was it about the car that they were interested in? Did the previous owner have outstanding tickets? Perhaps the tags had expired, he had never bothered looking at them. Or for some reason could they possibly be on to him. He had to be more cautious now, as he still had a few loose ends to take care of before he could flee the area. As it was, he would carry on with his current plans.

When they arrived at Roche Harbor, he exited the bus nonchalantly with the other passengers. The sun was out warming the area. Though there was a slight chill in the air it was acceptable. His jacket was keeping him comfortably warm. He walked past the small grocery store, down the wooden walkway and past the small post office and the laundromat to the end of the wooden deck area that overlooked the marina and anchorage area. The deck area here was lined with outdoor tables for customers of the small food vendor that was located just past the laundromat.

He stopped to get a soda pop at the open Dutch door of the food vendors, then settled at one of the green plastic outdoor tables, sitting in a position where he could see the parking area at the far end where he had departed the shuttle bus. He sat in the shade of the covering umbrella. Workers just to his right were working on an addition to the food vendor's shop. Just after eleven o'clock in the morning he walked back to the visitors parking area where he stepped into a public phone booth. He put the change from his pocket on the narrow shelf in the phone booth and dialed the operator. She, in turn, connected him with the newspaper. His conversation with the clerk was as short as he could make it, but he came away with a phone number and the name of Theodore Brewster.

While he had been in the phone booth, he had called the phone number she had given him. It upset him because he'd had to talk to an answering machine. He left a brief message and hung up. While making the call, looking out toward the marina, he made the decision as to how he would get off the island. Then he could get to the cabin to pick up his few clothes and his cash, then off to the mainland.

He went back to the vendor for another soda pop, then began to meander around aimlessly, or so it would seem if anyone should be watching him. The workers were gone for lunch so he walked innocently inside the work area that was covered with tarpaulins to keep the floors as clean as they could from the workers who had been installing new shelves and counter tops. Once inside he quickly spotted what he was looking for. He reached down inside the tool box, rummaged around until he found what he thought might do the job he had in mind. After he put the long hefty screw driver up the sleeve of his jacket, he walked out of the new building area and away from that part of the marina overlook.

HOME

Frank had actually gotten home earlier than usual, though he was only there to clean up a bit before he headed for Cary Ann's. When he got inside the door, he could see the small, flashing red light on his telephone recorder, he stopped to rewind it. Then as it started to play the messages he walked to the closet and hung his work jacket up, listening as he did so. He came to an abrupt halt and hurried back over to the recorder, rewound it, and listened to the message again.

"Mr. Brewster, I'm interested in taking you up on your offer for a game of chess if you'd like. I'll call again within a couple of evenings."

Frank turned the recorder off, looked at his wrist watch deciding he still had time to make the call and he dialed Ted's office. Ted's secretary answered and when Frank had told her who he was and that he needed to talk to Ted as soon as he could, she put him through immediately.

Ted was on the line quickly, "Yeah, Frank?"

"Ted, I'm sorry to bother you at the office, but my suspect in the chess killer case called and left a message on my phone recorder."

"And?"

"I'd like you to be the person he plays chess against." Frank had wanted to ask Ted to do this for him a little differently, but it had just come out.

"Whoa, partner, why me?"

"Because you're his chess equal or better."

Ted thought about it a few moments knowing Frank wouldn't let anything happen to him, then, "How is this game to take place?"

"I dunno yet. But I'll work it out so it's safe for everyone involved, okay?"

"Okay. Listen I've gotta go, I've got a client waiting for my counsel."

ROCHE HARBOR

As power boats of different, but manageable sizes came to the fuel dock, he would walk out onto the portion of the pier that overlooked the fuel pumps location. This was a location where he could hear the conversations between the dock master and the boat owners. The fifth boat that came to get fuel seemed perfect for his needs. While its tanks were being filled, the owner had asked, "You folks have any space open on the guest docks?"

"Yes, we do. How long would you be needing it?"

"Two or three nights, I think. We're spending a couple of days with friends in Friday Harbor."

"Okay, you see that space. The fourth one from the end out there?" He was pointing with his fingers.

"Yeah, that ones okay. Can I just pay for a couple of nights now as well?"

"Yes, sir."

"If I decide to stay longer, I can call you and let you know."

"Sure, that'll be fine."

He watched from his location on the overlook as the boat owner maneuvered the boat away from the fuel dock, out to the guest dock area and backed the boat stern first into the assigned guest space. As the owner of the boat was tying the boat up to the guest dock, he left his place on the overlook above the fuel dock and walked around the marina to the nearby hotel.

The hotel itself was old but apparently in good condition. Ivy was growing over the trellis that fronted the open deck area around the outside the hotel. The building's white paint shown brilliantly in the fading sunlight. The cannon's booming noise startled him as the local merchants started the evening ritual of taking the flags down. With the sound of the church bells ringing in the background he entered the hotel and walked to the low counter where a clerk waited.

"I need a room for the night."

"Did you want a bay view, or does it matter?"

"No. I don't need a view I just need a room to get some sleep." He thought for a few seconds then asked, "Is it possible to get a wake up call for really early in the morning?"

"I'm sorry, Sir. There won't be anyone at the desk from eleven o'clock until seven thirty in the morning. However, there should be an electric clock in your room."

"That'll work, thanks."

"Certainly, Sir. Sleep well."

She gave him a key and he registered as Jim Jones. He paid her in cash, picked up the key and found the stairs leading up. On the second floor he found his room, went in and quickly undressed for a shower. He hardly noticed the rich interior of the room and the old style of furnishings.

278

At two thirty in the morning, the alarm he had set woke him. He dressed hurriedly in the dark, quietly picking up the few things he had with him, including the large screw driver he had stolen from the workman's tool box.

He sat on the bed for a few minutes, listening. Satisfied with the quiet, he moved to his door, opened it slowly then he poked his head out and looked up and down the hallway. No one was around, and nothing seemed to be going on anywhere in the hotel. He slipped quietly out of his door pulling it closed behind him. He walked down to the end of the hall, then down the back stairs of the hotel. He opened the outside door and stepped through it into the dark. He was now standing on the back patio area of the hotel, almost tripping over a portable barbecue as he moved about in the darkness.

After letting his eyes adjust to the darkness he walked to the edge of the street running past the hotel, and looked both ways. Seeing no one around he quickly walked across the pavement and down the path through the open flower garden. On the other side he stopped again. He looked around the marina docks below him. Again all was quiet. He quickly walked out across the small bridge, turned right at its end, then proceeded to walk quickly down the guest docks.

Just before he got to the boat he had chosen he stopped to tie his shoe. This allowed him to look back the way he had just come. Nothing was in sight. He finished walking to the power boat he was interested in. He stepped over the highly varnished gunwale, then into the shadows of the fly bridge deck above the stern cockpit. With little hesitation he slipped the screwdriver between the locking hasp and the door. Two quick, hard jerks opened it. Inside the boat he moved to the control panel, fully expecting to have to climb under the panel and hot wire the switches. Instead he found the key in the ignition switch.

The diesel engine started easily and while it was warming up he turned on the instrument panel lights. A dull red glow allowed him to see the fuel tank was indeed full and the oil pressure gauge was climbing to the required position. As the engine warmed, he went out onto the deck, untied the bow line, throwing the line aboard. Then holding onto the side of the boat he went aft, untied the stern line and climbed back aboard. The stern line was now lying inside the cockpit, the boat sitting loose in the slip. Inside he pushed the lever forward engaging the transmission into forward gear. He let the boat idle very slowly out of the marina, he maneuvered without running lights turned on, out through the boats tied to mooring buoys and those anchored out.

The navigation between Roche Harbor on San Juan Island and Hunters Bay on Lopez Island had been torturous in the dark. It had taken him better than three hours to get here. Once he arrived deep into Hunters Bay, he anchored the boat in twenty six feet of water. After he lowered the boat's dinghy into the water from the swim platform, he shut the engine down. Just as daylight was breaking, he had landed on the beach nearby where he pulled the dinghy well up above the high water line and headed for the small cabin not far away.

From the cabin he could see if anyone came snooping around the anchored boat or the dinghy on the beach during the daylight hours. He couldn't be sure but he assumed the boat would be reported stolen before the day was out. He also knew he dare not move it during the daylight hours. If someone came around, he could deny any knowledge of it. After all he was a local resident.

OFFICE

Frank was just about to head to the coffee shop hoping to catch Cary Ann there, when his phone rang as he was pulling on his jacket. He picked up the receiver saying, "Detective Chambers here."

"Mr. Chambers, this is Sonny James. I'm with the San Juan Island Police Department at Friday Harbor. I've found a car I think you folks are looking for. It's a blue Ford, license number 123-ABC?"

"Yes, we are looking for that vehicle."

"We've got the car in our impound yard here on the island."

"Do you have the driver as well?"

"No. Sorry. We found the car on the incoming ferry, but we didn't find the driver and nobody's come forward to claim it."

"You probly won't have anyone claim it, either."

"What would you like us to do with it?"

"Hold it for me if you can and I'll have a team come have a look at it."

"You got it detective. Anything we should know about?"

"No. It's a case I'm trying to put together."

"Okay, we'll hold it for you."

"Thanks. I appreciate it."

"No problem."

While he was having coffee with Cary Ann, Jim came in, got some coffee himself and then joined them.

"Hi, Cary Ann."

"Hi, Jim. How have you been?"

"Fine, thanks."

Frank said, "How's your case coming along?"

"Just tied it up. The chief wasn't happy with the outcome though."

"Why's that?"

"One of our own may be involved."

"Oh, God! Not really!"

"Well, internal affairs will check it out. What appears to have been happening is this. A young woman would wait in her car until someone she had chosen would start to back out of a parking place at the mall. Then she would quickly drive her car in back of whomever was backing out, which resulted in her car being struck. She would jump out of her car as if very angry, ranting and raving. Whoever had backed into her would be in a state of shock.

She would then pretend to go call a cop. But then before he arrived or after he arrived, she would agree to settle on the spot for damage to her car. She would take whatever cash the person had and leave."

"How does this involve a police officer?"

"It would be her boyfriend who showed up on the scene. He might suggest that they settle between themselves if they could."

"Humm. Doesn't, sound good does it?"

"Nope." Then he added, "How's our chess killer case doin?"

"May have just gotten a break. The car we've been looking for is now impounded on San Juan Island for us."

HUNTER BAY

He hadn't seen a soul around the boat all day, at least, not when he was awake. He'd slept through the entire morning, then intentionally had taken naps during the afternoon so that he'd be well rested for the night that lay ahead. As the evening drew near he began to gather his meager things together, putting them, and the remaining cash, in a flight bag. He spent better than an hour wiping his finger prints off everything that he could think of, knowing he might not get them all.

Then, before he left the cabin, he left an envelope with enough cash in it for the next months rent, hoping the owner wouldn't be too upset over not hearing from him. He left a note explaining he needed to leave immediately and that he was sorry he had to do it without contacting him. What he was really doing was covering his tracks by trying not to offend anyone here on the island. He didn't want them raising any alarm concerning him because he was still going to be around for a while, or at least until he finished what he had set out to do. If the owner of the cabin was satisfied that something had come up and he had cash in his hands that he hadn't expected to get, he'd be content with the matter.

He'd waited until the sun had set and by the time he got all his stuff together it was almost completely dark, but now he was ready to leave. He stepped outside the cabin door. Before he left the cover of the front of the cabin he looked slowly around the area to see if he could see anyone who might be curious about him. Finally he walked down to the small boat still above the high tide mark, dropped his stuff into the dinghy and put the oars into the oar locks. Then he pushed the boat into the small surf.

He stepped into it and he sat down on the center seat as the small boat rocked gently with his weight. Settled, he rowed out to the power boat waiting at anchor. Once aboard the larger boat he started the diesel engine with the intentions of letting it warm up before he went forward. When the engine was warmed up, he went out onto the side deck. Walking forward on the narrow deck, he took his time moving to the foredeck taking care not to slip. On the foredeck the toe of his shoe found the switch seated flush into the deck. This switch he knew to be the foot button for the electric anchor winch.

The winch started pulling in the anchor line, but it suddenly pulled tight, as if the anchor was stuck under a rock. He operated the winch until the line was taut, then went aft and into the cabin. He put the engine in gear and moved the boat forward until he could feel the anchor pull out of the sandy and mud bottom. With the anchor free of the bottom, the engine's transmission was returned to neutral. As the boat drifted slowly toward deeper water with help from the offshore breeze, he returned to the foredeck and finished pulling the anchor up easily.

"Damn thing. I could've just cut it loose." He also knew there was always the possibility the anchor could be needed later, or it may not be. He stowed the anchor in its bow chock and worked his way back to the aft cockpit. Then into the main cabin. He put the engine in gear again, and at a slow speed he maneuvered out through Lopez Pass turning southeast toward lower Puget Sound.

Boat traffic was light as he traveled southerly down the water way. As he crossed Juan De Fuca he could feel some cross current as he started down Admiralty Inlet heading south. He passed an outbound ship, and about five minutes later he bumped across its wake. He felt he was in luck as he'd caught the incoming tide, which was helping speed him on his trip south. The tide helped carry him south so much that he slowed his pace when he was off Useless Bay so he wouldn't get to his destination too early.

A few hours later found him following the Seattle ferry into the Bremerton area. While the ferry made its way into its mooring slip and began to settle down he waited off the marina he'd been heading for, letting the engine idle as he drifted slowly. When the automobile traffic had left the ferry and before the waiting cars started to drive aboard, he turned the boat into the Bremerton Marina. He found an empty guest slip that he hoped would be okay for anyone to use without question. He shut the engine down after tying the boat up and turned all the running lights off, leaving only two small cabin lights on to see by.

Spending a few minutes, he began wiping his prints off the items he had handled while he'd been on board the boat except the anchor and he wasn't going to bother with that. He gathered his things together and turned the last of the lights off and left the boat, closing the sliding hatch doors behind him. At the top of the ramp leading down to the guest docks, he filled out a registration slip for the boat, putting it and enough cash for a week into the envelope. He slipped the registration envelope into the slot of the box for guests to use who came in late. He was certain no one would seriously check on the boat until the week was over

287

and more money was needed for the use of the guest slip. He casually walked away from the marina, then finally reached the main part of lower Bremerton. In a nearby twenty four hour market he found what he was looking for.

After leaving the market he stopped at a small restaurant that had opened at six A.M. for some breakfast. When he had placed the order for his breakfast he walked to the pay telephone on the rear wall and called the phone number. The phone rang several times before it was finally answered. "Hullo?" The person on the other end had no doubt been sound asleep.

"I'm sorry for waking you this early, but I read your advertisement about the Chevy on the bulletin board at the market."

The person on the other end of the phone line was now awake enough to make sense of what the call was about and responded. "Yeah, you interested in it?"

"Good! You still have it then?"

"Yeah, sure."

"It's just what I'm looking for, and I'll pay you cash in hand for it. Trouble is I'll need you to bring it to me."

"Where yah at." The chance to get the car sold before he was transferred to another naval base, now took over any thoughts of going back to sleep.

He explained where he was, yet the car's owner had seemed a little reluctant at first as he wouldn't have any way of getting home after he'd made the delivery. Finally the owner agreed to bring the car to him, when he explained he would also give him cab fare to get back home again, then he sat back down at the counter, his breakfast having just arrived.

FRIDAY HARBOR

Sonny James could hear the phone ringing in the distance while he held the receiver to his ear. When it was picked up on the other end, he heard a man say, "Detective Jim Parson."

"Jim, this is Sonny James, I'm with the San Juan Island police department. Is Frank Chambers around by chance?"

"Sure, hang on."

Sonny heard some scuffling in the background, then he heard Jim Parson's voice calling out for Frank Chambers, who was apparently not in his office but somewhere nearby. Suddenly, "He'll be right with you, Sonny." Then, it was quiet again as Jim put the phone receiver down again. A few moments passed, then the phone made a scraping sound as it was being picked up. "Frank Chambers here."

"Frank this is Sonny James. We talked a couple a days ago about that blue Ford we're holding in our impound lot for you folks."

"Yes, Sonny. I'm sorry my crew hasn't made it over there yet."

"Oh! Well that's not a problem. The reason I'm calling you now is because I may have something that ties in with this car being left on the ferry. At least there is a possibility it does."

"What's that?" Frank was looking for any lead that might go somewhere.

"Well, the coincidence of having found a car here that's wanted by you folks and a boat being stolen that same night, strikes me as a questionable situation."

"Hhmm, could be you're right! There could be a possible connection if someone was on the island but didn't want to be there, doesn't it?"

"Yeah, so I thought I'd call you and pass along the info on the boat we're looking for."

"Hang on, let me get some scratch paper and a pen." Sonny could hear a desk drawer open and close, then, "Okay, go ahead."

"We're looking for a 1992 Tolly Craft." He gave Frank the Washington registration numbers, a color description, the length, and when it was last seen.

"Anything else?"

"Well, while I was investigating the theft and checking around the area I found out there had been some guy hanging around the area all day. As a rule we're pretty used to boating enthusiasts watching boats come and go. Normally no one pays any attention to these folks because there's so much activity here with tourists. While I was in the marina area, I checked at the nearby hotel as well. You know, just asking about anything unusual, and it seems they did have one guest check in that day who apparently didn't stay the whole night."

"What's so strange about that? People often leave early."

"Well if it had been a man and a woman, probably not strange at all, but it was a man alone. The problem is this, if you decide not to stay all night where do you go? If you're driving, or on foot, you can't get off the island until the ferry's start running in the morning. Float planes don't fly out of here at night. Boats often leave, but not normally."

"So your consensus is the guy who stayed at the hotel, is the guy who took the boat?"

"Sure, well it fits the situation. I know you can't get off the island and I checked with the housekeeper how she knew he'd left early. She told me that when she made up the bed, she noticed that the alarm had been set for two thirty in the morning. She only remembered because of the odd hour. You know, after the bars close, and before anything else opens."

"Anybody give you a description of this guy?"

"Yeah, the woman who had him register into the hotel gave me some info. Let's see. . . . Ummm ,here it is, not much to go on though. Slender, with a small bald spot on top of a head of dark hair, paid cash for the room and signed in as Jim Jones. Nothing else to make him stand out. Then, of course, this might not prove to be the person who you, or I, are even looking for."

"I think that's exactly who we're looking for. I believe his name is Richard Evans. We want to question him in connection with several homicides here on the mainland."

"Bad dude, huh?"

"Bad yes, but I don't think he's subject to outbursts of violence. In fact I think he's a revenge killer. So he wouldn't be picking on anyone outside of his selected group."

"Well, if you turn anything up on the missing boat let me know will ya. I've gotten the word to the Canadian authorities already, so they'll keep an eye out over there, also the Vessel Border Patrol and Coast Guard, here and Canada as well."

"Sounds like you pretty well have it covered. On this end I'll notify the local Sheriff Patrol Boats as well."

"Thanks, Frank, I'll be in touch."

"Yeah, and I'll get that team over soon as I can for the Ford."

BREMERTON

He found the bus depot and left his flight bag in one of the small rental lockers. The key to the locker that held his flight bag, he then taped up to the inside top of another locker next to it. That key he put in his pocket. He'd taken enough cash out of his flight bag to last him a month or perhaps a little more.

After driving around town for a while searching for the right kind of location, he took a room at a small run down motel on the southern outskirts of town. The place was so old it didn't even have a paved driveway any longer. Even the gravel driveway had ruts well worn into it. The remaining white paint on the outside of the building had to have been at least ten years old, if it was a day.

Blackberry bushes hid most of the junk littered around the buildings from the view of the nearby main road passing by. The managers, if that's what they were, rented rooms by the hour, daily, or weekly. As far as he could see and for the most part, the motel was filled with migrant workers. The continual clamor of noise from the small children running and playing around the building and between cars was working on his nerves.

The first day he was in his room the hot plate had quit working so he had nothing to make coffee on. When he'd confronted the manager about it, the manager had reluctantly given him a newer one. He'd had to go to the store and buy some cleaning materials so he could clean up his own shower and the area around the toilet. He knew he wasn't going to get the best house keeping service here but he also knew this place wouldn't ask any questions of him either.

His new small pan, coffee pot and paper plates would suffice for a quick meal now and then, other wise he would eat out. He had found a plastic storage box to keep his coffee supplies and snacks inside of to keep out any bugs that might find them, and he bought a cooler.

He was glad he was driving an old car because more than once he'd found a couple of empty beer cans resting on top of the hood or trunk where the local folks had been leaning while drinking and talking amongst themselves, not caring about the condition of his car, or anyone else's for that matter. He knew he could put up with this life style a little longer, then he would go into business somewhere else in the country. He'd had enough business experience and luck over the years to have given him the good life. "I'll have it again. The nice cars, a large home and boats. Yes I will." He was thinking of times past. This next time he'd be more careful in choosing a wife so that his marriage wouldn't fail like the last two had.

He'd driven by Andrew Tatum's and Harvey Eldrige's places on two different occasions, but in both cases he'd spotted cars nearby at both homes with two men sitting in them. He couldn't be sure, but he'd suspected they might be police officers. "Is it possible that they're onto me?" He muttered out loud, but only to himself. "Nah. couldn't be. There's no way. They think I'm dead! Course maybe they suspect someone else, or something. Humm, I dunno." He was trying to decide if he should stay away from the last two names on his list.

He felt it was odd that there had been cars at both places with two men in them. Yet he wanted this thing finished. As he started driving back toward the motel, his headache had gotten worse, and he didn't want to put up with it. He turned the old Ford into a small shopping mall on the way back to his motel room.

Inside the store he picked up a bottle of aspirin and as he was approaching the druggist counter he spotted some free sample bottles of aspirin. They were small bottles of some new and improved type, but an idea had formed in his mind when he saw them. He picked up three of the bottles and put them in his pocket.

Before he left the shopping mall, he had purchased a small roll of aluminum foil and some very thin double sticky tape. The tape was the type that left only a film of sticky substance on a surface so you could put two items together without a space of some kind between them. He had another stop to make before he went back to the motel to work on his projects.

The next morning after he had gotten up, he gathered his latest wares together. A piece of the aluminum foil he'd torn off the roll was now spread out on his bathroom sink drain. He had already taken several pills out but now he took four more pills out of one of the bottles he'd used for his own personal use and very slowly administered the poison onto them. He'd had to do it slowly because he found that they would disintegrate if he did it faster. He had given them one coating of poison, then waited to see if they were going to crumble. They didn't, so he gave them another coating, then a third.

He pulled some tape off the roll and had just finished transferring the double sticky tape surface onto the sheet of foil nearby. Just as he was ready to pull the original foil covering off the tops of the other two sample bottles, the door to his room opened. Without knocking the housekeeper had unlocked the door to his room, stuck her head in saying, "Housekeeper."

Of course by then it was too late. When she saw him in the bathroom, she said, "Oh, I'm sorry I'll come back after while." Then she closed the door before he had a chance to say anything or even react to her intrusion.

Flustered he felt he had to hurry now. He knew she would return shortly and he didn't want to feel the need to explain what he was doing. He carefully removed the foil off the tops of the other two sample bottles of aspirin, then without further thinking he dropped two of his four doctored pills into each of them, then he put a piece of the new foil with the sticky tape on top of each sample bottle resealing each of them. With his pocket knife he carefully trimmed the edges of the foil off from around the rim of each sample bottle, after admiring his handiwork, he screwed the lids back on. He had just finished cleaning up his mess and thrown the remnants into a plastic bag, when the house keeper knocked on his door.

As he walked out of the door with a plastic shopping bag in his hand all he could think of was to say, "Would you change my sheets please?"

"Sure nuff, sugar. Gonna have company tonight, huh?"

He found a dumpster near the back of the grocery store where he dumped his sack of garbage. Then he spent twenty five minutes locating a library. When he got inside the library he spoke to the librarian and was given permission to use a computer with a word processor. The note he had written, and printed out, along with a twenty dollar bill was placed in an envelope and dropped into a drive by mail box.

He was afraid. Not for himself he thought, but for the facts he was having to face. He just couldn't see any way around it. If this idea didn't work, he was going to have to give up the game.

"I'm so close, so damn close." He knew there were only two more men on his list to take care of, which would finish his project.

That night before he drifted off to sleep on a bed that was well worn out and sagged badly in the middle, but he was satisfied that at least it had sheets and clean ones at that, he was thinking, "Maybe I'll play one game of chess across the board."

TRAINING

The chief had arranged for one of the senior
detectives out of Seattle to take one of their new
detectives out for a training session. Frank knew it was
something that the different departments did and as
his department wasn't training any new detectives, the
opportunity had been passed along to others.
Also, it would be a fun assignment for the new guy.

The training officer and the new trainee had spent the
afternoon out on San Juan Island. They had contacted
Sonny James when they arrived and he had taken
them to the impound area. Within minutes they began
their investigation of the Ford Frank had arranged for
them to check out. They stayed busy going through
the car from one end to the other but had little to show
for their efforts at the end of the day. When they
returned to Seattle a report was made out and the
results were sent to the chief of Frank's department
and ultimately to Frank. It read in part:

- -

THE AUTOMOBILE LICENSES NUMBER 123-ABC
A BLUE FORD MAVERICK WAS THE OBJECT OF
THE INVESTIGATION. VERY LITTLE EVIDENCE OF
VALUE WAS COLLECTED IN SAID AUTOMOBILE.
THE ITEMS OF SOME WORTH ARE AS FOLLOWS.
SEVERAL FINGER PRINTS WERE RECORDED;
SEE ATTACHED COPIES.
SOME HAIR SAMPLES ARE BAGGED IN THE
EVIDENCE FOLDER.
FERRY USE RECEIPTS (9) HAVE BEEN CHECKED
FOR PRINTS AND ARE BAGGED IN THE FOLDER.

- -

Frank was pleased with the results of the teams efforts and their ability to obtain some good finger prints. At least when he had a suspect in custody he had something that may link him to the Ford, which in turn would be a link to one of the scenes of probable murder. Finally he had something that could be used as conclusive evidence in a case that had been mostly circumstantial.

PATROL

It was after eleven o'clock at night. The two men were nearing the end of their shift. Both tired and cold and leaning back on the car seats which had been pushed as far back as they would go, leaving them with a little more leg room to stretch out. They had run the car's heater on occasion to fight off the cold and it helped but the warmth quickly escaped, bringing the cold back in a shorter time than they would have liked.

This had been a very boring stake out. Absolutely nothing had been going on. Bruno was catching a nap while Jake was supposed to be keeping an eye on things. Jake was close to dozing off, himself, when something happened. "Hey, Bruno, wake up." He whispered loudly while his right hand shook Bruno gently. Jake's face was still turned toward the house.

Bruno woke with a start, almost forgetting where he was. Rubbing his eyes, he said, "What?"

"The outdoor sensor lights at the Tatum's came on and I'm not sure, but I thought I saw someone running around the back side of the house."

"Dammit! I spose we better have a look see."

The two men took their flashlights and walked all around the Tatum property. A light was still shining through a window at the back of the house. So Jake said, " I'm gonna knock on the door and be sure everything is okay."

"Yeah, good idea, I don't see nothin in the back any where."

They walked back around to the front of the house, rang the doorbell and shortly a light came on in the entry way. A voice called out, "Who's there?"

"I'm sorry to bother you, Mr. Tatum. It's Jake and Bruno."

Andrew Tatum opened the door right away. He had come to know the men who were around his place at all hours of the day. Then as he spoke, something had caught his eye. Just as he said "What's up?" He bent down. "Darnn! Just a second, there's something in the way of the door."

Andrew Tatum came up with a sample bottle of aspirins in his hand. "Strange. I wonder where these came from?" He started to put them in the pocket of his robe.

Wary now and with no real reason to fall back on, Jake said, "You mean you didn't see those before now."

"No, I haven't. I suppose some ones going around doing a door to door sample delivery."

Because of the hour, and that someone had been near the house, Jake's first reaction was, "Mr. Tatum, would you just put that sample bottle into a plastic storage bag and let me have it?"

"Sure, sure," he said as his eyes looked up in surprise, puzzled over why the police officer had asked him for the sample bottle.

Shortly after he had been given the bag with the sample bottle in it, Jake and Bruno were about to get back into their car when their relief showed up. They passed the word on to them about what had happened, saying, "We'll take this back to the station for the detective squad."

HOME

Frank and Cary Ann were eating microwave popcorn that Frank had laced with some fake butter salt. The flavor wasn't bad, but it wasn't the real thing either. They were watching the late, late movie, eating popcorn and drinking cold milk. Suddenly Cary Ann jumped, startled as the phone near her rang. Frank reached over, picked up the receiver and said, "Yeah?"

"Franksorry to bother you this late. This is the night duty Sergeant at the station. Thought you'd like'ta know the stakeout team that was just relieved up at Mr. Tatum's house, brought in a bottle of sample aspirins that was delivered there sometime tonight."

"Why did they think they had to do that?"

"They said that when it was delivered, they saw someone running away from the house when an outside sensor light went on. Also, Mr. Tatum hadn't ordered any."

"Oh oh." Frank's alarm system went off inside his head.

"Yeah, so what do ya you want me to do with this bag?"

"Stick it on my desk, will ya? I'll take care of it in the morning."

He hung up the phone then without hesitating he dug his daily notebook out from his jacket that he had laid over a nearby chair. He opened the small notebook, turned a couple of pages, then while holding it open he

304

dialed the phone number he had found. It rang several times before a sleepy voice answered gruffly, "This better be important."

"Mr.Eldridge, this is detective Frank Chambers. I'm terribly sorry to wake you at this late hour, but I'd like you to do something for me. It'll only take a few minutes."

"My God, man. Do you realize what time it is?"

"Yes sir. I'm sorry."

"What is it you want of me?" He was beginning to wake up some now.

"Do you have a mail slot in your front door?"

"Yes I do, so?"

"Would you go take a look and see if there is a sample aspirin bottle there? If there is don't touch it. Just let me know, okay?"

"Just a minute." Frank heard some grumbling as the phone clunked down on the night stand, then silence. Moments later he was back. "Yeah there is one, how'd you know?"

"Would you pick it up with a piece of cloth and put it in a plastic sandwich bag? I'll have someone pick it up in the morning."

"Anything I should be afraid of?"

"Not if you don't open it and swallow any."

"Gotcha! That it?"

"That's it and thank you, sir. And goodnight."

He hung up the phone, turned to look at Cary Ann and said, "You wanna spend what's left of the night?"

"Sure, but what's going on?"

"Not sure yet, but I suspect my chess killer just made two attempts on the last two men involved in the tournament."

R			$\mathcal{B}$	K	B	N	R
P	P	P			P	P	
			P				P
		$\mathcal{P}$		$\mathcal{P}$			
		$\mathcal{N}$					
$\mathcal{P}$	$\mathcal{P}$	$\mathcal{P}$				$\mathcal{P}$	$\mathcal{P}$
$\mathcal{R}$			B	$\mathcal{K}$			$\mathcal{R}$

QP-QN4XN

OFFICE

Frank had the newspaper open on his desk and reading it. He was really concerned now because of the chess moves that had been in the morning paper.

He looked again.

10 QP-QN4XN ----- If = KXB
11 KXB ----------

He couldn't believe it, yet here it was. He understood exactly what was going on. The white Queen's Pawn moves up to the Queen's Knight four square, capturing his black Knight. This could have been an expected move. But offering an "IF" move, was what was unnerving. By making an "IF" move like this, the player was actually making two moves at once.

Frank knew that the killer didn't really care what chess piece his opposing player moved, in this case it was Frank himself. The killer was, in reality, announcing the fact that he had attempted to kill the last two players on his list at the same time. What he couldn't know was that Frank and his team had found out about the poisoned pills before any harm was done.

Frank left a message as to his destination with Sergeant Brown. He was taking the bottles of aspirin to the Criminalistic Department for a gas analysis. They'd be able to give him an answer about what was in the bottles for sure. Frank had gone out to lunch, then after his return he'd been waiting in the outer office of the lab for better than thirty minutes when the door to one of the labs opened.

A young man who didn't look old enough to even be working for a living motioned to him. Frank walked over to him and heard,

 "You Chambers?"

"Yeah."

"Come in detective, I think you'll find this interesting."

Inside the lab they walked through a maze of small cubicles, finally entering one larger cubical where there was a myriad of chemical equipment set up. On a small table he could see one of the aspirin bottles had been opened. "Watch what I do and I'll explain as we go along."

The Chemist explained to Frank that the bottles had already been checked for finger prints and that those prints had been recorded for him. Then with a small pair of stainless steel tweezers he began to peel the foil off the remaining bottle of pills. "You'll notice that this foil I'm removing is just a touch thinner than the foil used on most bottles sealing them against the elements and tampering."

Frank couldn't see it, but would take his word for it. Then the lab technician pulled the foil on the bottle the rest of the way off. He pointed to the underside of the foil, explaining as he picked up a medical swab.

"One of the things that I found of interest is the fact that the under side of the foil has a sticky substance on it. I suspect something like double sticky tape, but I'll run it through an analysis and provide you with that information as well."

He pushed the swab lightly against the foil and it was apparent the foil was indeed sticky as it held some fibers from the cotton swab. These items he put aside. He then picked the bottle up again and held it out to Frank to look at. "Look down inside and tell me what you see."

Frank looked into the bottle, then said, "I see two pills on top of some cotton."

"Exactly. But the pills should have been under the cotton from the manufacturer. This tells me that someone put these here and that person had to do so in a hurry. He, or she, as the case may be, overlooked the fact that the cotton would be covering the product."

The technician then dumped the two pills on top of the cotton out of the bottle into a small glass tray. "Let's go over here now," he said.

He motioned Frank to pull up a nearby stool. Then he sat down on the one near his equipment. The two pills were then submitted to the Gas Chromatography-Mass Spectroscopy analysis which broke the elements down into identifiable components. When the lab technician was done with the process and had the data he wanted, he reached for a nearby text book. He scanned through it briefly, then replaced it on the shelf, and picked up another book. After thumbing through several pages he paused in his reading. He was comparing his results to a computer library of standards.

"Here's what was in those pills." He showed Frank the text book name for a poison. To Frank it was a word that seemed about six words long.

"How deadly is it and how hard is it to come by?"

"Pretty deadly." Then he continued, "Actually, it's not hard to come by. I'll give you all the particulars in my final report."

"When will that be?"

"Oh, you'll have it in a day or two."

Back at the office Frank called Jennie at the newspaper, giving her his next advertisement. He wanted it to run right away and to stay in the newspaper throughout the weekend.

BREMERTON

He had gone to the bus station and gotten his portable chess set out of the flight bag, it was already set up before he even went out for the morning paper. Even while he was out getting the paper, he was impatient, but he waited until he'd gotten back to the motel before he read any of it. He sat on the edge of his bed and started looking at the first page to see if there had been any mention of anyone dying for any odd reason. He went on page by page looking for any indication of the deaths he knew should be there. He was disappointed when he didn't find anything. Wasting no more time he went right to the personals column.

There he saw . . .

10. NOT GOING TO PLAY THIS GAME ANY LONGER. PREFER TO PLAY ACROSS THE BOARD.

11. OR IS THIS TOO HARD FOR YOU??

He threw the paper across the room, pages flying in every direction. His anger about the lost championship game came welling up to the surface. He shouted out, "Who the hell does this bastard think he is!" He finally calmed down enough to get a cold beer out of the Styrofoam cooler that was full of cans of soda pop and beer covered with ice.

After he'd had something to eat later in the day he was restless, he paced half the night away with worry. Many thoughts were running through his head. "I can beat this guy easily." And, "I should move on and start my new life." Finally he had made the decision he needed to make. He'd take this brazen chess player on in a chess game and teach him a lesson and then

He'd get on with his life. With this decision made he got into bed and slept deeply.

TED BREWSTER

It was just after seven in the evening when the phone rang. Frank picked up the receiver and said, "Yeah?"

"Mr. Brewster?"

The hair on the back of Frank's neck began to raise. He felt the adrenaline rushing through his system. He knew who this was on the phone. "Yeah! Who's this?"

"This is Patrick, your chess opponent from the newspaper."

"Ahh, Patrick, my fellow chess player, good to hear from you."

Richard was trying to sound nonchalant, instead of angry. "So you're interested in a game across the board are you?"

"Only way to really enjoy a game with a qualified chess player such as yourself."

"When would you like to play?"

"Suit yourself." Frank didn't want to come across sounding like he was in a rush.

"Well, it'd have to be soon, because I'm about ready to leave on an extended vacation."

"Well, if you'd rather not play me?"

Richard could feel the anger welling up again, but contained it. "Actually I'm not sure you're a qualified opponent for me."

Frank laughed. "I suppose I had that coming, didn't I?"

Now Richard relaxed. "Yes, yes you did. Tell me what's a good time for you?"

Frank didn't want him coming here to his own apartment, but he'd considered an alternative plan anyway. "Tell you what. I play an open board at the Main Library in Everett on Tuesdays and Wednesdays. You know, where anyone can come in and sit down to play against me."

"I could drive up to Everett for a game. Which day would you prefer?"

"The choice could be yours. However, Wednesday is usually pretty busy. There are a few college kids who think they can kick my butt. That's the day they come in."

"What time?"

"Suit yourself. I'm there from about seven till nine P.M.. Come in as you like."

"Maybe I will, maybe I will. Keep a board ready."

He hung up thinking, 'I'll be there, but it'll be me who kicks your butt.' Later he became concerned briefly because of the others who had met their deaths by his hand in the close proximity.

OFFICE BRIEFING

Frank had them all in his office right after lunch. They were going over the plan once again. "Okay, listen up." When they were all paying attention, he said, "It could be Wednesday, but I'm putting my money on Tuesday. So, tell me again what each of you are going to be doing tomorrow night."

The chief had reluctantly given Frank permission to use two people he wouldn't normally be able to use. Ted Hyakawa, because he was to be the chess player in Franks place because he was the one who could effectively play the man they were after. Frank had convinced the chief, that this man they were after would see right through Frank's game immediately.

The other person Frank wanted to use was Cary Ann. One reason was that she had kept her police qualifications up to standard, and because all but one other police woman was involved in cases where they couldn't be pulled away on such short notice.

Frank pointed to Ted and waited. Ted looked slightly embarrassed because of his roll in this situation. "I'm going to be sitting quietly reading a chess book, while waiting for any opponent to sit down to play me a game." He paused, then added, "Then if things get hairy I'm gonna duck under the table!" The others chuckled.

One by one they went around the room. Cary Ann explained how she was going to be a library helper who would appear to be putting books away on nearby shelves. Then when they were sure their man was in the area, Cary Ann would go to the book check out area and help process people out of the library and would not let anyone else inside. In a sense, locking the library.

Jim would be sitting in a nearby reading area with a copy of some latest magazine of some sort. Jim would actually make the arrest, as Frank distracted their suspect just near the end.

Michelle was the one undercover policewoman to be used and she was going to be roaming the area looking for books as if she were involved in a research project of some sort. She would be piling one book on top of another at a nearby table as she found what she was looking for.

After they had discussed their roles in this setup, Frank asked. "Cary Ann, you're going to be in a dress, correct?" Frank asked.

"Yes, should I come armed?"

"I don't think it'll be necessary."

Then Frank continued, "Michelle, you're wearing jeans and a sweatshirt is that right?"

"Yeah, and I'll have a loose wind breaker on as well. It'll help my cover as I'm gathering books for a research project."

"Ted?"

"Casual. Jeans and a light shirt."

"And I'll be wearing jeans and maybe a sport coat." Frank said, then "Jim, what about yourself?"

"Probably a sport coat and slacks. It seems that the rest of you will dress sloppy, so I'll add some class to the group."

Frank grinned at Jim's comment. "Okay, any questions about how it'll go down?"

They had talked about it several times exploring every possibility, each of them knowing it would actually just take place naturally.

"Okay folk's that's it for the day, I guess, unless any of you have anything you want to go over again. Everyone looked at everyone else and they all shook their heads side to side indicating, no they didn't. They all left but Frank who had another phone call to make.

He looked for the number in his Rolodex and dialed it, smiling, as he waited. "It was close now. So close."
 The phone rang twice before it was picked up on the other end.

"Sonny James here." Frank heard.

"Sonny, Frank Chambers here. We found your missing boat this morning."

"The hell you did!"

"Yes, we did. Also we found prints in her that match the prints lifted from the Blue Ford you held for us."

"Where's the boat at?"

"It's at the marina in Bremerton. You want us to contact the owner, or do you want to get in touch with them?"

"I'll call him. It'll look better from the tourist angle."

"Okay by me, Sonny."

"What kinda condition is it in?"

"Looks pretty good. Although it had a broken lock hasp on the door going inside."

"That's great, Frank, and thanks."

COMPETITION

They were stationed around the area, trying to look like regular library patrons. The librarian knew what was taking place and she would hurry her customers along without being obvious. Cary Ann was working back and forth, saving one portable tray of books to be put away. These books were primarily for the area near Ted's location. Frank was the only one who was really staying close to Ted. Jim was milling around the library keeping an eye out for a man who fit their suspect's description.

Ted, who had a chess board set up, was reading a chess book and was actually engrossed in it. He was the only one who seemed comfortable with the situation. Seven o'clock came and went. They were all getting nervous except Ted who was showing some impatience. Frank was just thinking that perhaps they should pack it in for the day, when Jim dropped some magazines at the end of an aisle.

Frank looked up and saw Jim shift his eyes toward the doorway. Behind Jim, Frank saw a man sauntering in their direction. Cary Ann had seen him as well. She was ready with her cart, but held back. The man seemed to be nervous, yet with a comfortable stride as well. Slowly he worked his way over to the table where Ted was still involved in his book. The man looked down at the board calmly saying, "You interested in a game?"

Startled, Ted looked up, smiled and said, "Sorry, I'm saving a game for a friend." Then as if having thought it over, he said, "Oh well, go ahead and sit down. He's late anyway."

Richard Evans pulled the old oak chair out from the table and sat down. The white pieces were on his side of the chess board, but he reached out and picked up a white pawn, then a black pawn from Ted's side as well. Putting them behind his back, he mixed them up, back and forth, from one hand to the other. With a Pawn concealed in each hand he pulled his hands back in front of him offering Ted the choice. Ted smiled and chose the man's left hand. It was a black Pawn. They didn't have to change the board.

"You Ted?" his opponent asked as he moved the Queen's Pawn to the Queen's four square.

"Yeah, you must be Patrick?"

"Richard grinned, saying, "How'd you know?"

"Only an experienced chess player would open with the Queen's Gambit."

Richard was relaxing somewhat now, as he watched Ted reply with his chess move. When Ted moved his King's Knight to King's Bishop three the game began to get serious. He and Richard were both now involved in the game, oblivious to the world around them. The minds of both men were engaged in serious mental combat.

After they had played a few moves, Ted could see he could be checkmated in a few short moves if he wasn't extremely careful. Frank got up and moved slowly over to the end of the table where the game was going on.

They both looked up at him and he said, "Do you mind if I watch?"

Richard Evans said nothing, he was a little apprehensive, but Ted answered for them, "No, just don't talk to us while we're playing, okay?"

"Okay." Then Frank sat in a chair near Ted leaving an empty chair between the two of them and at a slight angle across from Evans. Frank was trying to size Evans up. He felt comfortable after watching him for a few moments.

Michelle had been standing behind a bookcase that was also right behind Evans, now she was staying closer to the end and farther away from Jim, who was just out of eyesight of Richard Evans, and to his left.

Richard had just made a move that placed Ted's game in jeopardy. He had taken one of Ted's Rooks, and opened an attack on two other key pieces.

Frank gambled and said, "Good move, Richard."

Richard replied, "Yes, it could be the deciding move."

"Well, it's not over until it's over," Ted said.

Richard finally realized what had happened. That he had been called by his real name and that he had answered to it. He almost bolted, but he looked at Frank, who was smiling at him. He knew then he'd been set up.

Ted looked up at his opponent and said, "They're here to arrest you."

Jim was behind Evans now, and as Richard stood up Jim took one hand, pulled it behind his back slipping a hand cuff on the wrist. The other arm came back voluntarily. Richard knew there was no way out. He was now aware of the two policewomen and the two detectives who were surrounding him. He looked down at Ted saying,

"You're kind of a sore loser aren't you?"

"You haven't beat me yet."

www.ingramcontent.com/pod-product-compliance
Lightning Source LLC
Chambersburg PA
CBHW051235260626
47162CB00002B/434